This book belongs to

_____

Children's
POOLBEG

BUGSY GOES TO
LIMERICK

First Published 1988 by
Poolbeg Press Ltd.
Knocksedan House,
Swords, Co Dublin, Ireland.
This edition 1990

© Carolyn Swift 1988, 1990

ISBN 1 85371 014 8

Cover design by Judith O'Dwyer
Printed by the Guernsey Press Ltd.,
Vale, Guernsey, Channel Islands.

BUGSY GOES TO
LIMERICK
CAROLYN SWIFT

Children's
POOLBEG

Contents

For my granddaughter Lena, with love

High but not Dry
Who Knows Why
A Horse Will Shy ?
A Ghost Goes By
A Curlew's Cry
A Chance to Fly
More than Meets the Eye
Never Say Die
You'll Never Miss the Water
Till the Well has Run Dry

1

High but not Dry

ate Masterson jumped out of bed and ran to look out of the window. It was raining again and the raindrops striking the surface of the Grand Canal made the water look as if it were boiling. All the fish should be well and truly cooked by now, Kate thought, considering how many days it had been raining.

This morning, though, the rain did not matter for today was the day she had been looking forward to for weeks. At last, she and Bobby were going on tour with the company, instead of being dumped on Aunt Delia for the summer holidays.

Until now, she had always wondered why her friends at school envied her for having parents who worked in the theatre. It had certainly meant that she could sometimes get tickets for shows without having to pay for them, but that did not make up for having to go to Aunt Delia's every summer.

Aunt Delia was their mother's elder sister, who lived in their grandfather's old cottage in the foothills of the Dublin mountains. At first, it had been fun going there. Kate had enjoyed surprising rabbits on the mountain tracks and picking blackberries from the hedges. But Aunt Delia always expected her to work and while Kate never minded collecting the eggs, she hated bringing in the goats. And she did not much like the taste of goats' milk either, even if it were supposed to be good for you.

Born and brought up in Dublin in one of the little red-bricked houses laid out in rows between the South Circular Road and the canal, Kate was very much a city girl. She found the slopes of Kilmashogue full of frightening sounds at night. As for Aunt Delia's goats, they had black bodies and white faces, so that when they suddenly appeared through the evening mists, their horned heads loomed like threatening evil spirits. Worst of all, Kate always knew that while she was with Aunt Delia, she was missing all the fun the others were having and would talk about when the company got back to Dublin.

Having parents in the theatre had been no fun at all up to now, Kate thought. It was different for Bobby. He had got a small part in *Bugsy Malone*, when it was produced in the Olympia one Christmas, while Kate had been too young to audition for it. So now Bobby felt he was in the same league as his parents and Kate had to listen to his endless stories of the trials and triumphs of show business.

He had only had a small part as a member of Dandy Dan's gang, but at the time he had talked of nothing else, until his father started teasing him by calling him "Bugsy". Somehow the name had stuck and now all the company called him that, but Bobby did not mind. Kate thought that she would not mind either, if they would only give her a part in a play too. For the first time Bobby now had a part in the play the company was taking on tour and Kate had made such a fuss at the idea of going to Aunt Delia's on her own that she was being allowed to go too.

"Bobby! Kate! Are you getting up?"

Their mother's voice came from downstairs and Kate heard the springs of Bobby's bed creak as he rolled out of it. For once, there would be no need to shake him, Kate thought, as she ran to reach the bathroom ahead of him.

Her mother set her boiled egg on the table as Kate came into the kitchen.

"Sit down and eat," she said, "I've no time to waste this morning."

"What time are we going, Maggie?" Kate asked. She and Bobby had always called their mother and father by their first names.

"Pat and I will be leaving the minute Chloe gets here," her mother said. "Pat's just loading the car now."

Kate knew that was only her mother's way of putting it. Jim Dolan would be doing the loading, while her father watched and gave orders.

"Mind that tape deck," he would say unnecessarily. Or, "Take care of those amplifiers. I can't afford to replace them if anything happens to them."

But Jim would take no notice. He was well used to Pat Masterson by now, for he had been Pat's stage manager ever since Kate could remember. Suddenly Kate realised that Maggie had not included her in the reply.

"But how am I going?" she asked, suddenly fearful that she might end up at Aunt Delia's after all.

"In the van with the scenery," Maggie told

her. "Chris will pick you and Bobby up around ten. You'll have to lock up, so make sure all the windows are properly closed before you go, won't you?"

Kate nodded. She felt glad to be responsible for something. She was even more glad that they were going with Chris MacSweeney. He was the youngest member of the company and, in Kate's opinion, much the nicest. He had only joined them a few weeks earlier, after Pat had seen him playing in Listowel during Writers' Week. Chris was only starting a career as a professional actor, but his dark curly hair and blue eyes were just right for the part of Lawrence Scarry.

Donal was supposed to have been playing it, as he had done in Dublin. Then he had been offered a part in a new RTE television series and he had asked if he could be replaced for the tour. Kate had watched her father run through his whole acting range. At first he was the powerful boss, threatening to see that Donal never worked again if he broke his contract. Then he became the defeated champion, let down by his only remaining supporter, begging Donal not to desert him. Donal had just waited for the performance to end. He had been with the company long enough to know that in the end Pat would give in. He would understand the temptation for a young actor to earn bigger money and the chance of being seen by many more people, And of course, in the end, he had agreed to let Donal go if he could find a suitable actor to take his place.

It was then that Pat remembered Chris. When he found that Chris was not only free to take over the part, but had also once driven a milk van for the local co-op, he made up his mind. Chris was engaged to play the part and act as assistant stage manager under Jim Dolan.

Until then, Jim Dolan had always had to drive the heavy van that held all their scenery, costumes and essential props. Now he would be free to go on ahead with the Mastersons to set up the sound system and check out the furniture and set dressings that the resident stage manager would have got, working from the list that Jim had sent down to him.

"Am I late, darlings?" The deep, slightly husky voice gave even such a simple question the thrill of melodrama.

"There's Chloe now," Maggie Masterson said. "You can tell Bobby his egg's in the pan.

It must be nearly hard-boiled by now, but that's his fault." And she hurried off to greet their leading lady.

Kate knew her father and mother sometimes laughed at Chloe Kennedy behind her back, imitating her grand manner, but Kate thought she was beautiful. Having neither dark hair nor blonde herself, but something in between the two that Bobby unkindly called "mouse", she envied Chloe the red-gold hair which fell softly around her shoulders. Even more, she envied her graceful sweeping gestures, for Kate sometimes felt she had more arms and legs than she quite knew what to do with.

When she was small, she had followed Chloe around like a puppy and had been allowed to sit on a chair in Chloe's dressing room while she put on her make-up. And Kate had watched everything she did very carefully, so that she knew exactly how Chloe made her green eyes look much bigger than they really were, and how she used highlights and shadows to stress her high cheekbones, giving her a mysterious and slightly eastern look.

"I don't know why Chloe had to get up so early," Kate's mother had said, "*She* doesn't have to get to Limerick in time to check the advertising and arrange newspaper interviews. She could come on later with the others."

"Can you imagine Chloe travelling with the scenery?" Pat had replied, laughing. "She would think it beneath a leading lady to travel in a van. Besides, she's probably hoping if she comes with us she might get her photo taken with me!"

Kate pretended not to hear them. Chloe was always kind to her. Anyway, she was glad Chloe was going to travel by car. If she had been in the van, Chris would have talked to her all the time.

Kate was relieved when the old black Audi finally set off. There had been the usual last minute panic, of course. Pat had mislaid the leather briefcase with the scripts and Maggie had told her at least three times to make sure the front door was double-locked but, in the end, they had gone, leaving Bobby and herself to wait for Chris and the van.

"Chuck over the bread," Bobby ordered, lounging back in the kitchen chair. "No sense in leaving it after us to go blue-mouldy."

"You'll bust if you eat any more," Kate objected.

"You should stoke up too," Bobby replied, "we don't know where or when we'll get to eat again."

"We can eat whenever we like," Kate said, "Maggie left us a packed lunch and anyway we'll be in Limerick in time for tea. If you don't hurry we'll never get the breakfast things washed up and put away before we go."

"Plenty of time!" Bobby said, but they were only just ready, with the delf washed and their bags in the hall, when Kate saw the grey van come round the corner of Lennox Place onto Portobello Road.

"I'll sit in front," Bobby announced, pushing ahead of Kate and climbing into the passenger seat.

"So you will, Bugsy, and Kate too," Chris agreed, "for I couldn't squeeze a day-old chick into the back beside that skip. Unless either of you fancy riding to Limerick seated on top of it."

Kate looked at the big wicker hamper holding the costumes and knew the backs of her legs would show the marks of the basket weave long before Limerick.

"I'd rather sit in beside you," she said.

"In you get, so." Chris held wide the driver's door so she could slither in next to Bobby and then he climbed in after her. Switching on the windscreen wipers, Chris drove around the block, crossed the canal at Portobello Harbour and followed the far bank until he turned left onto the dual carriageway.

"Have you been to Limerick before?" Kate asked him when they were well on the road, wondering what sort of place was to be their home for the next week.

"I have, to be sure," Chris grinned. "Haven't you to pass through it to get anywhere you'd want to be going?"

"You mean, to get to your own home, don't you, Chris?"

"And to Tralee and Listowel and Killorglin."

"What sort of a place is it, then?" Bobby asked.

"A fine big city, Bugsy," Chris told him, "on the River Shannon."

"But I thought we were going to the country," Kate said in surprise. "Are there no mountains there?"

"Not in the middle of O'Connell Street, that I ever noticed," Chris laughed, "but there's Keeper Hill not twenty minutes' drive away and that stands over 2,000 feet. Limerick's ringed with mountains the very same as Dublin."

"I don't know why you didn't go to Aunt Delia's if it's mountains you want," Bobby muttered. "I don't care if I never see another mountain as long as I live."

"I like them except when it's getting dark," Kate said.

"You'll have your fill of mountains before the tour's ended," Chris told her. "I'm only thankful we're not playing half-ways up them, like I did last year. But your mother has booked us into fine theatres, God bless her."

"Pat doesn't play in halls now he's famous," Bobby boasted.

"And why would he?" Chris said, as he pulled up for the traffic lights in Newbridge. "Didn't he have his fill of that over the years? It's a grand company he has now and I'm lucky to have landed work with him. If I can only make some sort of a fist of the part he'll maybe keep me on after the tour."

"He won't pay you, except when you're playing or rehearsing," Kate said. "He doesn't do that, even with Chloe."

"He can't afford to," put in Bobby. "There's no money in theatre in this country."

"Your mother's very words to me, Bugsy," Chris said.

"Of course," snapped Kate. "Where d'you

think he heard them? But if Pat thinks you're good, he'll ask you back again and again. He likes to have the same people in the company."

"That's right," agreed Bobby. "He says you're always better off with the devil you know."

Kate did not know why Chris found this so funny, but he was still laughing as they passed the Curragh race course and he only stopped as he slowed the van coming into Kildare.

"Whether or no," he said seriously, "I really hope I can make a go of the part."

"Are you nervous?" Kate asked in amazement, for Chris looked as if he would never be afraid of anything.

"Why wouldn't I be?" he said. "Lawrence Scarry's hardly off the stage all night. It's the biggest part I've ever had, since I was an amateur, that is."

"Well, I'm not nervous," Bobby boasted, "and I'm playing the stableboy for the very first time."

"Ah, but it's different for you, Bugsy," Chris told him. "There's no-one going to sack the boss's son."

"Anyway, he's only got two lines," Kate said. "Though I'd be nervous even so, if it was me."

"Well, it's not," Bobby said flatly, putting Kate down as usual. "How could you play a stableboy?"

"Couldn't it just as well be a stablegirl? It wouldn't make a scrap of difference to the play!"

"They didn't have stablegirls in those days, silly. When that play was written, girls only did things like sewing and cooking!"

"But it isn't just this play," Kate complained. "None of the plays Pat does ever seems to have parts for girls!"

"Cheer up, Kate!" Chris took his left hand from the wheel for a second to give her shoulder a quick squeeze. "You'll get your chance one of these days, you'll see!"

It was still raining as the van headed for Birdhill nearly four hours later. They had stopped to eat their packed lunches just outside Toomeyvara, where there were lovely white-painted picnic tables and seats on a grassy lay-by. Now the tables all had little puddles of water on them as the raindrops spattered the shiny surface. All they could do was to look at them through the misty windscreen, as they sat in the car drinking their minerals and the bottle of beer that Chris had bought in Roscrea.

"There are your mountains now," Chris said to Kate, as they left Nenagh behind them. Set back a few miles from the road, the mountains loomed mistily at them out of the haze of rain on their left.

"Are we nearly there?" Kate asked.

"Another half-hour should do it easy, if the traffic's not too bad drawing in to Limerick," Chris said. "We've made good time so far, thanks be to God. It will do me no harm at all with your father to arrive in good order and on the early side. I suggest that we .... "

He broke off sharply at the sound of screaming brakes. Ahead on their right, an ice-blue Ford Sierra had shot out of one of the old country roads, now half-hidden behind a lay-by, and skidded in a right-angled turn on to the slip road.

"Silly eejit!" snarled Bobby. "If that lay-by hadn't been there he'd have come straight out on to the road and .... "

"Look out!" screamed Kate. But she was too late. The car, instead of stopping, had continued to the end of the slip road and swung sharply to its left, its brakes screeching once more, as it plunged straight out across the road in front of them.

Cursing, Chris braked sharply. As the

offending car disappeared down a steep hill to
their left, the heavily-laden van skidded on
the wet road surface, sloughed across the soft
margin and ended up with the near front
wheel high up on the ditch.

Chris wiped the sweat from his forehead.

"I thought for a moment there that our next
appearance would be in heaven," he said. "Are
ye both all right?"

Kate nodded wordlessly. For a second she
had felt a cold shiver of fear right between her
shoulder blades. Then she had been flung
forward on to the dashboard, before slithering
sideways and ending up in a heap on top of
Chris, with Bobby on top of her. It was
amazing that none of them had been hurt.
Now she felt as if she might be sick.

Chris groaned as he realised how steeply
the van was angled.

"And I just after congratulating myself on
making such good time," he complained.
"Wouldn't it have to be me on the spot when
some maniac goes looking to kill himself? Say
a prayer there's nothing broken in the back, or
there's no knowing what your father will do to
me!"

Bobby looked at the bushes on the ditch,
doing their best to push their way in through

the closed window beside him.

"We're not going to be early now," he said. "We're right up on the ditch, and it's going to take us all our time getting down off it!"

2

Who Knows Why?

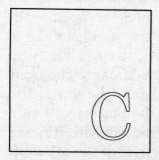hris buried his face in his hands. "It's only the mercy of God she didn't keel right over," he said. "What the hell was that madman at? He could have killed the lot of us!"

"He must have been in a desperate hurry," Kate said. "Did you see the man with the black moustache looking at his watch?"

"I was too busy trying to avoid hitting him to be studying his movements," Chris said savagely. "We'd better see if we can right her."

The van was so far up on the ditch that even the driver's side was raised up into the air. Chris opened his door and jumped down on to the muddy margin below the ditch.

"Well," he said, "at least nothing's going to run into us. We could hardly be further in off the road."

Kate pulled up the hood of her anorak and clambered down after him. Her shoes squelched in the mud as she landed. The rain was still coming down in sheets and it was no time for standing around on the open road. Still, if there was trouble she would not like to leave Chris to face it alone. He was already up on the ditch inspecting the damage. The front of the van had ploughed into the top of the ditch and the wheel on the passenger's side was deeply embedded in the soft soil. He gave it a tug or two and then gave up the attempt. Bobby yelled from the van to ask if they needed any help. Kate thought he did not sound very eager. It was hard to blame him. The rain had already darkened her anorak from pillar-box red to crimson and a little rivulet of water was running down Chris's face from a straggle of hair on his forehead.

"We'd want to lift her out of it," Chris said. "Either that or drag her out. Either way, the three of us would never manage it. We'd want a few strong lads to shift her."

A car tore past them on the crown of the road, sending up a fine spray of muddy water.

"We should have flagged him down," Kate said. "He might have helped us."

"Don't waste your breath on dead embers,"

Chris told her. "He was going too fast. Never look for help from a man on a runaway horse. What we need now is a tractor."

"We passed one a mile or two outside Nenagh," Kate said hopefully. "He could be along soon."

"More likely he turned off miles back. If we could get a lorry even, there might be a lad or two with the driver for unloading."

"Then we'd want to be ready to stop him," Kate said. "I'll stop the ones going this way if you hold them up on the other side."

"Mind yourself then," Chris warned, "and don't stand too close. They'll give you a shower if they don't run you down!"

He crossed to the lay-by opposite, but in a few minutes he was back again.

"Get into the van, for pity's sake, girl! You look like a half-drowned kitten! There's none of them going to stop in a downpour. They've no mind to get wet any more than Bugsy there. There's a house over beyond on the old road. I'll run across and see can I get help there."

Kate obediently hoisted herself back into the van beside Bobby.

"You were a great help!" she said.

"No sense getting soaked for nothing,"

Bobby retorted, sliding along the seat to avoid contact with Kate's wet anorak. "When there's something useful to be done, I'll do it."

Then Chris was back, looking more bedraggled than ever.

"The woman of the house is there on her own," he told them. "But she says I'll get help in Cappadine."

"Where's that?" asked Kate.

"Down the bottom of the hill to our left, she says."

"That's where the car went!" Kate exclaimed.

"I'll not see hair nor hide of that," Chris grunted. "At the rate that car was going it could be halfways to Cork by now — if it's still in the one piece, that is!"

Kate and Bobby watched him set out and disappear round the corner just ahead of them.

"We're going to be late now," Bobby said gloomily.

"I hope Pat doesn't give out to Chris about it," Kate said. "After all, it wasn't his fault."

"That won't stop Pat yelling at him," Bobby told her. "He hates having to set up and light the show in a hurry."

"It's not fair," Kate said. "We were in great

time until this happened. Maybe if Chris gets help now we may not be too late."

"You don't know how long it takes to set up!"

"Nor do you!"

"I know how long it took to rig *Bugsy*."

"That's different! We've nothing like the big sets they had in the Olympia. You're just showing off again!"

"I'm not! I know how long these things take, that's all!"

Kate said nothing. When the show had opened in Dublin, she had sat among the empty seat rows in the darkened theatre, waiting for the dress rehearsal to begin, but of course it was different for Bobby. Even if he only had a two-line part, it was his show. And it was worse for Chris. As assistant stage manager he would be involved in getting the stage ready. On top of that, he had a big part. And he wanted Pat and Maggie to be pleased with him. A late arrival would hardly help.

She gave a sigh of relief when Chris appeared, followed by three men. They walked to the front of the van, inspected the wheel and then rolled up their sleeves.

"Out ye get!" Chris called to Kate and Bobby.

Tumbling out on the roadside, they were

delighted to find that the rain had almost stopped. A few isolated drops and the spray from passing cars were all that was left of the downpour. A burly, fair-haired man who seemed to be in charge climbed on to the ditch, followed by one of the others.

"Are ye right?" asked the man. Chris nodded and took up a position on the other side of the van with the third man.

"One, two, three!" said the burly man and to Kate's astonishment they lifted the van, heavily laden though it was, clear of the ditch and set it back on the roadside. Kate clapped her hands.

"I never knew you were so strong," she said to Chris.

"There's the man you should be saying that to," he laughed, nodding towards the burly fair-haired man, who was wiping the mud from his hands. "He had to lift her out of the mud and she was well stuck!"

One of the other men grinned.

"You had the right man for the job," he said. "There's great strength in a miner."

Kate looked again at the fair-haired man. Neatly dressed in grey trousers and pullover, he was not in the least like her idea of a miner.

"Are you really a miner?" she asked.

He smiled at her, and little creases appeared at the corners of his twinkling blue eyes.

"We don't wear the tin helmets on a Sunday," he said. "And you needn't be giving me all the credit. The weight of the load was tilted on to the other side."

Chris had unlocked the back of the van and was inspecting the contents.

"Well, thanks be to God," he sighed with relief. "There looks to be no great damage done. It was packed too tight to shift. If we get going we might have it up in time for the dress rehearsal yet!"

"You in the theatrical business then?" the fair-haired man asked, looking curiously at the scenery stacked in the back of the van. Chris nodded.

"And if we have the set up on time it will be thanks entirely to you," he said, relocking the back door. "We open tomorrow night in the Belltable and if you'd like seats you'd be more than welcome. The play's *Shanwalla* by Lady Gregory and it's about the doping of a racehorse. It takes place in this part of the world, too."

"I don't know now," the man said. "Not looking the gift horse in the mouth or anything, but by the time I'm cleaned up and had the bit of tea I'm not much in the humour for the drive to Limerick. You'd be fairly done in after the day's work," he added apologetically. "Maybe on the Saturday night, if you'll be there then."

Chris looked embarrassed.

"We're not supposed to give out free seats on a Saturday," he said awkwardly. "It's the one night we can be nearly sure of a full-house, like. I could ask, seeing that you saved our skins, in a manner of speaking, but . . . ."

"Not at all!" The man seemed anxious to put Chris at ease. "The missus couldn't have come anyway, on account of the babby. But I've a child about an age with this pair and I thought it might have made a bit of an outing for her."

"Would she mind watching a rehearsal?" Kate chipped in. "Because, if not, you could bring her along tonight."

"I'm not sure would your father thank me for bringing anyone to the dress," Chris said uneasily.

"I wouldn't say he'd mind if she didn't talk," Bobby commented. "He let Kate and I bring along friends to the dress in Dublin. But she'd have to put up with the hanging about. There are always hold-ups at the dress rehearsal," he added, turning to the fair-haired man to explain. "It's getting the technical stuff right."

"She could sit with me," Kate said, thinking it would be nice to have company. "That way I could explain everything to her."

"I'd have to come too," the fair-haired man pointed out. "There's no way of getting there and back only by car. And I wouldn't want a stranger lifting her. You'd never know who'd be on the roads these times, and there's a five-mile walk from the main road to the cross."

"But I thought you lived just down the hill," Kate said.

"Ah no," the man told her. "I'm only visiting the cousins in Cappadine. I live over at Silvermines."

"And is that where you work?" Kate asked.

Chris looked surprised.

"But I thought the mines had been shut down," he said. "I remember seeing a programme about it on the telly a year or two back."

"That was Moghul," the man said. "I was with them right enough. But when they shut down I began work at the open-cast mine across the road."

"Well," said Chris, opening the driving door and gesturing to Kate and Bobby to get back in, "you'd be more than welcome. It's not a bad show, though I daresay it's not for me to be saying it!"

"Mary'd be only made up seeing it. Won't she be boasting to all her friends at school how she met these play actors down from Dublin and saw them practising their play?"

"Then we'll see you later. I don't know what time we'll get started in the heel of the reel, but you'd want to be there by half-eight to be on the safe side. You can ask for me, Chris MacSweeney."

"Right," the man said, as Chris climbed back into the driving seat. "And my name's Joe Casey."

Chris leaned down from the van and shook his hand, before slamming the door and turning the key in the ignition.

"Goodbye, Mr Casey, and thanks a lot," Kate called politely, waving, and Bobby waved too as they set off for Limerick once more.

*   *   *

Before they even reached the front of the theatre, Kate could see Maggie waiting impatiently for them outside.

"What in the name of God kept you?" she

shouted, hurrying over as Chris drew up at the curbside. "Pat's up the walls!"

"I'm sorry, Maggie," Chris began, but she cut in, without listening to his explanation, with directions to drive the van around to the back of the theatre. "Jim and the resident stage manager are waiting there for you for the past hour!" she added. "And you two, get out quick! I'll drop you round to the digs. The car's across the road and I'll be in trouble if I leave it there a minute longer!"

Then she hustled them away, with a final shout to Chris: "And for heaven's sake get that set unloaded before Pat has a seizure!"

As the car edged through the traffic in O'Connell Street and around the one-way system on to Sarsfield Bridge, Bobby and Kate told Maggie what had happened, but it did not have the effect on her that Kate had hoped.

"I suppose I should have had more sense than to let Chris drive the van," she said. "Your father thought we'd save time by bringing Jim with us to get things going, but I might have guessed it wouldn't work!"

"It wouldn't have mattered who was driving," Kate told her. "The car came straight across in front of us. If Chris hadn't pulled up real fast we could have crashed!"

But she might as well not have spoken for all the notice Maggie paid to her.

"When we get to the digs you're both to get unpacked and be ready for tea the minute Mrs Harris calls you," she went on, pulling up at a garden gate a little way up the Ennis Road. "And you can tell her not to bother about tea for us. We can always grab something in town later. Come on, get out!"

And before Mrs Harris had even opened the front door Maggie had pulled out into the traffic again and was gone.

"You'll be the Masterson children now," Mrs Harris said by way of welcome. "Come on in, till I show you your rooms."

As she led them upstairs, she never stopped talking for a single second. It was as if she were afraid something terrible might happen if she paused for breath.

"Your father and mother always stay with me any time they're in Limerick," she said. "It must be ten years or more since I first opened that door to Pat and Maggie. Many's the time I asked them why they never brought you along with them. Don't you know well, I said to them, that you can trust me to mind them as if they were my very own, and wouldn't it be better than leaving them with their aunt? But what harm? Aren't you here now and more than welcome."

She stopped suddenly at the top of the stairs and turned abruptly to face them.

"Wasn't there supposed to be another lad along with you?"

"Chris is down at the theatre unloading the set," Bobby explained. "We were late arriving so he may not be here till after the dress."

"And Maggie said not to be cooking tea for her and Pat," Kate added, suddenly remembering her mother's final instructions. "They haven't the time to get back and they can get something later in town."

"They'll do no such thing!" Mrs Harris cried indignantly. "Don't they know well I'll not let them go hungry? I've a bit of cold ham and a tomato for Jim when he comes in to his supper and Pat and Maggie and the other lad can have the same. I hope the lad won't mind going into No. 3 with Jim and yourself and I've put you in here on your own, young lady."

On the last words, she flung open the door of a small room off the landing with no number on the door.

"It's not really a bedroom, but I thought you wouldn't mind, seeing that it's only for the one week."

Kate looked at the couch that was playing the part of a bed and at the little desk that was acting as a dressing table. Then she knelt up on the chair and looked out of the window onto the street beyond the fence and the little garden.

"It's lovely, Mrs Harris," she said. "Thank you very much for fixing it up for me."

Mrs Harris beamed. "You're a grand little girl, God bless you!" she said. "And you'll be no trouble at all, I can see that."

"Why does she get a room to herself when I'm the one that's in the play?" Bobby complained.

"Well now, I didn't like to ask Miss Kennedy to share. She's in No. 1 as usual and . . . ."

"Pat always has the No. 1 dressing room in the theatre, not Chloe," Bobby argued, but Mrs Harris was having no nonsense of that sort.

"We've no stars in this house," she said firmly. "And No. 1 is the only single room. Pat and Maggie are in No. 2, the way they always are, and three's the largest room we have. I often put a camp bed in there for families."

"Don't mind Bugsy there," Kate said, imitating her father. "He's just showing off!"

"And you're just jealous!" retorted Bobby.

Mrs Harris laughed.

"I'll have no fighting in this house or star complexes either. You'll be wanting to get cleaned up for tea. I'll have it for you in ten minutes."

Kate shut herself into her little room and tipped the contents of her tote bag out on to the bed. She would put on a clean tee-shirt for their guests, she thought. It would never do for the miner's daughter to be telling all her friends at school that the play actors down from Dublin were a scruffy lot.

She had it all done in a flash and Mrs Harris had not yet called, so she lay down for a minute or two on the little bed, to try it out. She closed her eyes and saw again the friendly face of the miner. Suddenly the image was replaced by the face of a man with a black moustache and a wolfish smile like a snarl. As the man glanced down at his wrist watch, his face seemed to sweep across her mind like a picture sweeping across a television screen. She felt again that little cold shiver between her shoulder blades, remembering how he had crouched in his seat like a tiger, ready to pounce on its prey.

"Why am I thinking about him?" she asked herself. "It's over. Over and done with. I'll never see him again now."

But even as she heard Mrs Harris calling from downstairs that the tea was ready, the face of the man with the black moustache came back into her mind and she knew it would come back to haunt her in bed that night and maybe the next as well.

3

A Horse Will Shy

ate sat at the end of the second row of seats in the darkened auditorium and waited for something to happen. On stage, Chris, already made-up and dressed as Lawrence Scarry, the stableman, was moving around from one pool of light to another, according to her father's instructions.

"Now," her father's voice called from the back of the theatre, "can you angle that spot outside the window so it hits Chris where he's sitting now?"

A man she had not seen before appeared through the door in the set carrying a step ladder, crossed the front of the stage and disappeared on the far side where there was no door. There came the sound of metal scraping on metal. Then a silence.

"What's happening?" her father cried

impatiently.

"Hang on a minute!" came a voice from somewhere backstage. Then the soft blue moonlight jerked abruptly to the right.

"How's that?"

"It'll do!" Pat said grudgingly. "All right. Go on to the next cue."

A young woman came down beside the seat rows and spoke into the darkness to no-one in particular.

"There's a man out front asking for Mr MacSweeney," she said.

"That will be Joe Casey," said Chris, getting up from the chair.

"Stay where you are!" yelled Pat Masterson and Chris sat down again.

"I'll go," Kate said. "It's for me really," and she followed the young woman out through the swing door at the back of the auditorium. Her father's voice called after her: "All right, but don't bring them in here if you're going to talk!"

Joe Casey was standing looking at the outline of a man's head in green brushstrokes that was part of an exhibition of paintings in the theatre foyer. Beside him stood a girl in a brown dress, her red hair loosely tied in a pony-tail. They both turned as Kate came towards them.

"This is Mary," her father said, and Kate noticed she had the same smile as he had.

"They're not quite ready inside," Kate explained. "And we can't talk in there. Let's sit in the wine bar so we'll know when they're starting."

"I might slip out to Gleeson's for something stronger," Joe said. "I'm not much of a man for the wine."

"You can't even get wine tonight," Kate said. "The theatre's not really open, you see."

"I don't mind," Mary said. "I'll stay here," and she went with Kate into the alcove beside the empty bar counter.

They sat in silence for a little while as Mary looked curiously about her.

"Were you never here before?" Kate asked.

Mary shook her head and Kate wondered suddenly what they were going to find to talk about.

"Did your father tell you how a car nearly crashed into us today?" she asked finally.

"He did, and how it nearly went off the bridge."

"There wasn't a bridge," Kate began, but Mary corrected her.

"There is! Right by my uncle's house. Over

the Kilmastulla." And, seeing Kate still looked puzzled, added: "The river that runs into the Shannon below Killaloe. All the streams on our side of the Silvermines Mountains go into that."

"D'you live in the mountains then?" Kate asked.

"Near where my Dad works. The mine workings are in the side of the mountain."

Kate was becoming more interested.

"I've never seen a mine," she said. "They sound very exciting."

"They're not," Mary said discouragingly. "You can't get into Moghul, where my Dad used work, and where he works now is only like a big quarry. The only underground mines you can see are the old workings up the mountains and some of them are hundreds of years old."

"They sound sort of spooky."

"Most of the shafts are concreted in so you can't see them at all. Or else they have netting round them to stop people falling down them. Anyway, they're all full up with water now."

"I'd like to see them all the same," Kate said. She had always been curious about everything, driving Pat and Maggie mad with her questions. There were so many things, she thought, that you read about or saw on the telly, that you never ever got to see for yourself. And she never felt she really knew about anything unless she had been able to touch it or smell it or taste it for herself.

"I'd take you to see them," Mary said, "only there's no bus to Silvermines from Limerick except on a Saturday morning."

"Maybe Maggie would run me over in a day or two when she isn't so busy," Kate said.

"D'you think she might?" Mary sounded excited herself now.

"Maybe. If Bobby would come too."

"That's your brother, isn't it? The one that was with you in the car. Isn't he here now?"

"You'll meet him after the show. He's in the dressing-room just now, getting ready."

In fact, Bobby was not getting ready at all. He needed hardly any make-up to play the stableboy in the small Belltable and it had taken him only a few minutes to get into his costume and darken his skin a little so that he looked as if he spent most of his time outdoors.

Since he was not on stage until the third act, he had meant to go into the auditorium as soon as he was ready and watch the first two acts. Then he remembered that Joe Casey and his daughter would be there and he decided to stay where he was. He was not in the mood for being polite to strangers, particularly strangers who were not in the habit of going to the theatre. For all his boasting to Chris, he was just as nervous as he was and the long wait for his entrance only made it worse. He hoped the Caseys would not hang around after the show. He did not want to have to talk to them about it.

"I wish we could get going," he said aloud.

"I know how you feel, Bugsy," Chris said, "It's easier when you've something to be thinking about. You can give me a hand to hang the bridles if you like. At least the stage management keeps me busy."

"Will the play be starting soon?" Mary asked Kate out front in the wine bar.

"The minute they're ready," Kate told her. "I did warn your Dad you'd have to hang around a fair bit."

"That's all right," Mary said. "I don't mind. And I hope you come over to see us. When will you know if someone will lift you?"

"I'll ask after the rehearsal," Kate said. "It's no good talking to anyone about anything now. They'd only say to be quiet."

"We could have fun," Mary said.

Kate said nothing. Bobby had protested

that morning that he never wanted to see another mountain as long as he lived. Most likely he would refuse to go. And maybe he was right. If the mines were really boring, she thought, it could be embarrassing. She did not know what to talk to Mary about. She went back to the only thing she could think of.

"Did your father see that car go over the bridge then?" she asked.

"He did not, but he heard it. He was having a cup of tea inside in the kitchen and heard it go roaring down the hill. That's how he knew it was strangers, he said. No-one around here would come down the hill like that".

"I always think people drive faster when they know the road," Kate said.

"Not when they know how steep the hill is and that there's a hump-back bridge and level crossing at the bottom, just around the bend. There was a desperate screech of brakes when the car hit the bridge and they'd never have had time to stop before the level crossing gates. They'd have been closed only for it was Sunday."

"Why?" Kate asked.

"To keep the animals from wandering on the tracks," Mary explained. "Nobody uses the old roads now except on a Sunday to go to mass.

Then the gates are left open. Even though it's miles nearer to go to our house that way it's quicker to go by the main road."

"That car must have been lost so," Kate said.

"Da said he thought they'd turn back when they saw the grass growing in the middle of the road beyond the tracks, but they kept on going."

"They were in an awful hurry," Kate agreed. "Even after they nearly hit us, the man was looking at his watch."

Suddenly, the auditorium door swung open and Maggie Masterson came out.

"We'll be starting in a few minutes," she called to Kate. "You can bring your friends in now if you like."

"What about your Dad?" Kate asked Mary. "Will I run down to Gleeson's?"

Mary shook her head.

"He'd have said."

"Come on, then!"

The two girls went in through the swing door and took their seats in the middle of the fifth row. The house lights were up now and taped music was playing, as if the girls were a real audience. Maggie came back in and sat beside them, just as the lights and music faded and the curtains parted to show an old harness room, with bridles hanging on the wall and a blind beggar sitting by the fireside.

"That's my Dad!" Kate whispered to Mary, but her mother glared at her so she broke off before she could explain that the woman sitting beside the table sewing was really Chloe, no longer looking mysterious and oriental, but just like the wife of a stableman might have looked a hundred years ago.

Kate had already seen the play so, unlike Mary, she was not worrying about what was going to happen. She was only anxious that Chris would be good as the stableman who refused to be bribed. Seeing him on stage while they fixed the lighting, she had thought he looked better in his costume than Donal had done, but Pat and Maggie would want more reason than that to keep him in the company.

"Those that are blind should see ghosts more clearly than those that have their earthly sight," Chloe was saying. "I've heard tell that one of the master's grandfathers still haunts this place."

"Aye," said the blind man that was really Pat Masterson, as he groped for the edge of the table to put down his drinking mug. "Many a one has seen him galloping through the woods, sitting up straight on his white horse, with his huntsman behind him in his red jacket."

"There was a woman from the North told me once," Chloe continued, "that whenever you see a tree shaking there's a ghost in it."

"Is it a ghost story then?" Mary asked Kate in a whisper.

"Sh! You'll see!" Kate whispered back, for she had heard Chris off stage whistling, and knew that meant it was time for his entrance. Then he raised the latch on the half-door and strode to the centre of the stage, calling:

"Is it you, Owen Conary, keeping the woman of the house in talk?"

He sounds good too, Kate thought. Not a bit nervous. He was on stage then right to the end of the first act, except for the few minutes when he was supposed to have gone to draw water from the well. When the curtain closed on him, kneeling beside the body of his dead wife, Kate turned to her mother.

"He's good, isn't he?" she asked.

"He's all right," her mother said. "But it's early days yet. Wait till he's over the jealousy scene in Act 2. That's where he's weakest."

It was odd, Kate thought, as the house

lights came up for the interval, the way she was almost as anxious as if she were in the play herself. Tomorrow night, when the audience was there, she knew she would be really jumpy. She felt glad and sorry at the same time that it was not herself waiting backstage for the curtain to go up again. Then Mary nudged her.

"The black fellow murdered her, didn't he?" she asked, but Kate would only say: "I'm not telling." There was no point in spoiling it for her by giving the whole plot away.

"Anyway," Mary said, "it's the end of her!" But Kate only smiled, knowing Chloe was in the dressing-room at that very minute putting dark shadows under her cheekbones and white powder on her face, ready for the moment near the end of the second act when she would slip onto the stage in the place where there was no door and only the blind man would see her.

Maggie Masterson looked at her watch.

"They'd better get their skates on," she said, "or we'll be running into overtime. It must have been well after nine before we got started. I'm going to see what's holding them." And she mounted the steps at the corner of the stage and disappeared behind the curtain.

The swing door at the back of the auditorium opened and Joe Casey came in.

"Is the play over?" he asked the girls.

"Ah, no," Kate reassured him. "You only missed the first act," but Joe looked at his watch.

"I don't want to be late getting back," he said. "I've a day's work ahead of me tomorrow."

"Ah, Da, we can't go yet!" Mary said. "It's just getting exciting!"

"I'll wait awhile so," he said, sitting down beside his daughter as Maggie Masterson reappeared from backstage.

"Right! We're going now," she called, and the house lights began to fade even before she reached her seat.

When the curtains parted to show the brass candlesticks with their guttering candles and bottles and clay pipes scattered everywhere about the room, Joe Casey looked at them with interest.

"They've had a death in the house," he commented. "Mind you, it's not today nor yesterday I last saw pipes smoked at a wake!"

But Mary sat in silence as the stableman, full of grief and alcohol, fell a prey to the scheming O'Malley, just as Shakespeare's

Othello was tricked by Iago. Remembering her mother's words, Kate was delighted that Chris looked truly drunk and his anger seemed real as he cried: "My seven curses on him and on his house and upon his soul!" But then, a few minutes later, he seemed to falter and she heard quite clearly Joe's voice giving him the first words of his next speech.

"It's well pleased I'd be to see the horse sunk in the bog below," Chris began. Then he stopped and corrected himself. "I mean, sunk in the river below or smothered in the bog."

"Keep going!" snarled the beggar impatiently and quite out of character for a blind man who had just asked haltingly: "Is there anyone within?"

"I'm sorry, Pat," Chris said, equally out of character, "but I just don't believe Scarry would say that. I mean, he loves that horse. I don't think however much he wanted to be revenged on Darcy he'd think of taking it out on the horse!"

"It's too late for thoughts of that kind now," Pat snapped. "You're not going to tell the audience that tomorrow night, are you? Just say the lines so we can all get on with the play!"

"Sorry, Pat," Chris said again and went

back to his talk of revenge but though Mary
caught her breath when the ghost appeared,
Kate waited anxiously for the second interval.
Surely Chris knew better than to argue with
her father in the middle of a dress rehearsal?

When the lights came up, Joe Casey clapped
enthusiastically and stood up.

"That was fine play-acting," he said, "and
I'm thankful to young Chris for inviting us."

"But it's not over yet," Kate told him.
"There's still the last act."

"Maybe so," Joe said, "but it's time we were
heading for home."

"Ah no, Da," Mary protested. "Kate's
brother still has to do his part."

"And the last act's quite short," Kate added.
"There's a good bit cut from it, you see, so we
need only have one girl and one policeman
instead of two of each."

"Well," said Joe reluctantly, "if you're
starting again right away . . ."

"As soon as they change the set," Kate
nodded. "They just have to strike the harness
room and set up the magistrate's office."

"And will that take long?" Joe asked,
preparing to sit down again.

"Ah, no," Kate began, but her voice was
drowned by the sound of a crash, followed by

angry voices from backstage. Pat Masterson's voice, trained to carry to the back of the largest halls, topped them all.

"How many times have I to tell you never to cut corners like that?" he demanded. There was an inaudible protest, cut short by Pat again.

"Well, you *should* have had the time, if Chris hadn't been late getting here."

Kate looked worried. Why did he have to keep picking on Chris? Maggie Masterson swept through the door beside the stage like a storm sweeping in from the sea.

"They'll have to fix that flat before we can go on," she said. "We'll definitely run into overtime now."

"We'd better go so," Joe Casey said.

"I'm sorry," Mary whispered to Kate, "but he hates to be out late when he's on the early shift."

"Can't be helped," Kate said.

"But you'll still come out to us?" Mary pleaded anxiously.

"I don't know." Kate hesitated, glancing at her mother. "I don't know how I'd get there."

Maggie looked impatient. "What is it you want?" she asked.

"Mary wants me to go to her house — when

the show's running, of course."

"I'd lift her myself," Joe Casey added, "only I'll be at work."

"How far is it?" Maggie asked, her mind on the hammering backstage.

"Off the main road to Nenagh. You'd do it in half-an-hour easy."

"Nenagh?" Maggie frowned, trying to focus on the problem. "Pat and I are invited to lunch at Rathboy House on Tuesday. That's somewhere near Nenagh, I think."

"Is it Toddy O'Connor's place at Kilriffet? That's not above two miles from Silvermines."

"Where Mary lives," Kate explained, seeing the vague look on her mother's face. "She's going to take me to see the mines if I can go."

"Not that there's anything to see," Joe muttered. "They're all concreted in to prevent accidents."

"In that case I could leave Kate and Bobby over on my way to lunch and collect them on my way back," Maggie said. "They can bring sandwiches."

"Indeed they will not," Joe said warmly. "If they won't mind taking a snack with Mary and the Missus. We don't have the dinner till I get back from work."

"That's very good of you. We'll be out around

mid-day on Tuesday. Where are you exactly?"

"Just around the corner from the chapel. Anyone will tell you where Casey's is."

But Mary whispered to Kate: "You won't need to ask. I'll be looking out for you," before she hurried off to catch up with her father.

It was as well they left when they did, Kate thought afterwards, because there seemed to be an age of hammering and cursing before the curtains opened on the third act and her mother's fears of going into overtime were well-founded. It was half-an-hour after midnight when the curtains finally closed on an unhappy-looking Chris, standing on the opposite side of Chloe to her father and bowing to token applause from her mother and herself.

So bad did everyone feel about the way the rehearsal had gone that, driving back to the digs for their cold supper, it was left to Kate to whisper across the back seat to Bobby that he had been fine as the stableboy. In the front of the car, Pat and Maggie were too busy raking over the mishaps of the evening. As they crossed Sarsfield Bridge, Maggie suddenly broke off.

"Look out, Pat, it's a guard!" she warned.

Peering out through the steamed-up

window, Kate saw the dim figures of two uniformed gardai up ahead.

"If it's not one thing it's another!" groaned Pat, jamming on his brakes, as the garda on their side of the road flagged them to a stop. "I'm in no humour for answering a lot of silly questions about licences and insurance."

"Whatever it is, try to keep your temper," Maggie whispered. "If you annoy him it will only take longer."

Pat swore under his breath.

"I can see this tour is going to be one long disaster," he said, as he wound down his window to face the garda.

4
A Ghost Goes By

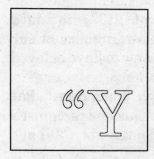

es?" Pat Masterson asked, with ill-concealed impatience. "What's the problem?"

The young guard looked at each of them in turn and then seemed to lose interest.

"Where are you from?" he asked casually, as if he had to say something.

"Dublin," Kate's father replied tersely.

"And you saw nothing unusual like on the road?"

Seeing the look on her husband's face, Maggie Masterson intervened quickly, before her husband could vent his ill-humour on the representative of the law.

"We came down from Dublin earlier in the day," she said. "Now we're on our way back to the digs from the theatre, where we've just finished rehearsing for the play that opens there tomorrow night."

The guard looked at them with new interest, finally concentrating his attention on Pat. Then he relaxed.

"Mr Masterson, isn't it?" he said respectfully. "You gave a performance at our school one time. I'm sorry now to have delayed you."

"Only doing your duty, I suppose," Pat grunted. As always, when someone recognised him, his temper improved noticeably. "What's the trouble anyway?"

"Been an art robbery over near Ballina. We've road blocks set up right around. Well, I won't keep you from your beds any longer. I hope your play does well for you."

"Thanks. I hope you get your robbers. Goodnight now," and Pat wound up the window and drove on.

"Where's Ballina?" asked Kate suddenly.

"Just across the bridge from Killaloe, if you know where that is."

"I mean, which side of you would it be if you were driving from Dublin to Limerick?" Kate persisted.

"On your right. Now, stop asking silly questions. Your father's tired."

Bobby gripped her arm.

"I know what you're on about!" he whispered. "That car! You think that's why they were in such a hurry, don't you?"

Kate nodded. "D'you think we should go back and tell the guard?"

"Dad would kill us if we asked him to turn back now. Besides, that was hours and hours ago. The robbers could be on the boat to Holyhead by now."

"We ought to tell someone," Kate insisted.

"Let's wait till the morning," Bobby said. "Dad will have calmed down by then. It can't make much difference after all this time."

All the same, Kate said to herself, kneeling up on the chair in her little room for a last look out of the window before she switched off the light, what would the guards think if the robbers got away because they were afraid to annoy Pat? But then they would never guess how awful he could be when he stopped being the charming, friendly leading actor and began to imagine that they were all against him. Look at the way he had rounded on poor Chris!

"I'll never sleep for worrying about it," she said to herself, and then fell asleep almost before she had finished saying it.

*   *   *

Next morning, she dressed quickly and went down to the room beside the front door where Mrs Harris was ladling jam from a pot into little bowls, one for each table.

"Well, aren't you the early bird?" Mrs Harris exclaimed when she saw Kate, "and you not back till all hours!"

"Did you hear anything about a robbery last night?" Kate asked anxiously, by way of reply.

"Indeed and I did," Mrs Harris said. "Wasn't it on the news this morning? How they got away with it I don't know, and all the burglar alarms and guard dogs they had about the place!"

"I think we saw the robbers," Kate told her, "and maybe we should tell the guards about it."

"*You* saw them?" Mrs Harris stopped ladling jam and stared at Kate. "Well, for pity's sake! When was that now?"

"Yesterday, on the way here. They were in a car that nearly crashed into us."

"Children!" laughed Mrs Harris. "You wouldn't be up to them, the things they can think up!"

"We didn't imagine it, honest!" Kate protested. "The car put us right off the road and up on to the ditch. Ask Chris if you don't believe me!"

But Mrs Harris only laughed again and went on ladling jam.

"I'll not argue with you about that," she said, "but there's many a bad driver that's not a robber. Your car had nothing to do with last night's break-in. That didn't happen till near midnight. It's all there in the paper if you want to see for yourself."

Kate took the paper from the sideboard, beside the funny little cottage made out of delf. The big black headlines were right at the top of the front page.

PRICELESS PAINTING STOLEN FROM HOME OF WEALTHY BUSINESSMAN, she read.

"Where does it say it didn't happen till midnight?" she asked.

"Further down the page," Mrs Harris told her, screwing the top back on the jam jar.

Kate glanced at the double column of print beside a photo of a big house on the edge of a lake. Under it was a line of heavy print and Kate read that too: **Inchamore House, where last night's robbery took place.**

"Sit down and read it properly," Mrs Harris said, as she put the last of the little bowls out on the table in the window. "You may as well, for I'll be a few minutes cooking your fry."

Kate folded back the right-hand side of the page so the paper would fit on the table between the plates and sat down to study it.

"Mr Patrick Flynn," she read, "the well-known car-hire magnate, was assaulted last night in an armed raid by four masked men at his Georgian mansion on the shores of Lough Derg near Ballina. They tied up Mr Flynn, his wife and staff, before removing a painting by the famous Spanish artist, Francisco Goya, believed to be worth four million pounds.

"The gang entered the house undetected, despite the presence of guard dogs in the grounds and an elaborate alarm system. The robbery, which took place shortly before midnight, was not suspected until Mr Flynn succeeded in freeing himself some twenty minutes later and alerted the Gardai, who immediately threw a cordon around the area, which covers the borders of counties Clare, Limerick and Tipperary."

That was it then. Mrs Harris was right. The man with the black moustache who had looked at his watch as the car hurtled by them could have had nothing to do with the robbery. While she waited for breakfast, she finished studying the newspaper report.

"The Basket Seller," she read, "is 28" by 30"

and was painted in 1779 when Goya was 33, as a companion piece to *The Crockery Vendor,* completed the previous year and now in the Prado Museum in Madrid.

"Gardai consider the robbery to be the work of professional criminals with a knowledge of art, or working in collaboration with art experts, since paintings of lesser value were left untouched. The gang would, however, have considerable difficulty in disposing of a painting so well-known, since it would be recognised immediately it appeared on the art market."

Kate had just begun to read the interview with a farmer, who had been up all night with a cow that was calving and had told the gardai he had heard a car speeding in the direction of Ballina some time after midnight, when Chris joined her at the table. He looked so unhappy that Kate forgot all about the robbery on the spot.

"Don't mind the things Pat said last night," she told him. "He's just nervous too. He'll be different tomorrow if everything goes well tonight."

"And suppose it doesn't?" Chris replied, looking gloomily at the plate of rashers and eggs that Mrs Harris had brought him.

"Suppose he thinks my performance is desperate?"

"He won't!" Kate said soothingly. "And Chloe always says a bad dress rehearsal's lucky! It means you'll have a good first night. When things go wrong at the dress you've time to put them right. Maggie says that's what a dress rehearsal's for."

"She said different last night," Chris said, "And more than her prayers too!"

"She was only worried about having to pay overtime rates," Kate reassured him. "She says touring costs so much now that there's never any money over to cover anything extra. I'd hate to be a business manager and have to worry about the cost of everything. I'd much rather act."

"Acting's not all it's cracked up to be either," Chris said. "You worry about forgetting your lines and you worry about getting bad notices. And as if that's not bad enough, you're paid so little you still have to worry about the cost of everything!"

"Why does everyone want to be an actor so?" Kate asked.

"Ah!" Chris shrugged. "If you knew that you'd know everything."

"But you must know why *you* wanted to! You

could have stayed with the co-op."

"I could if I'd half the sense of a sparrow. It's a class of a madness comes over people, the wish to be an actor but once a man sickens with it he'll never over it. If you're wise, you'll look for the day-time job when you finish your schooling."

"Maybe so," Kate said, "but I'd like to see if I'm any good at acting first."

Chris shook his head and then, hearing Pat Masterson's ringing tones echoing down from the landing above, buried himself behind the paper Kate had been reading.

Kate waited till she was on her own with Bobby to tell him what she had learned about the robbery.

"Now aren't you glad I didn't let you ask Pat to go back last night?" he said at once in his maddening, older-brother voice.

"But the man in the car looked so like a robber!" Kate protested.

"Robbers can look like anything," Bobby said. "It's only on the telly you can always spot the baddie by the way he looks."

"But the car was flying!" Kate said. "D'you think maybe they were on their way to the robbery?"

"Of course not. They wouldn't have been

racing if they were. They'd have been quiet as mice so nobody would notice them. Anyway, if they had been they'd have got there hours too soon."

Kate knew he was right. What's more, from what her mother had said, the car was going the wrong way.

"But why . . . ." she began.

"Oh, forget it, will you!" Bobby snapped and Kate realised he was as edgy as Chris and her father. Theatre people were really no fun at all before a first night, she thought, and for the first time she understood why she and Bobby had always been sent to stay with Aunt Delia. Now, not being in the play herself, she was the only outsider and no-one wanted to talk to her.

Luckily, Mrs Harris talked enough for all of them. No matter how busy she was, she had time to answer all Kate's questions and had plenty of questions of her own as well.

"Isn't it a wonder Miss Suttle never married?" she said, as she put dirty linen into the washing machine. "D'you think she might make a go of it with that new lad that's with you now?"

"D'you mean Chris?" Kate asked in horror.

"The curly-haired Kerry lad."

"Of course not!" Kate was indignant.

"Chloe's old!"

Mrs Harris started to laugh again. Why did everything that Kate said seem to make her laugh?

"Not too old to turn a young fellow's head if she'd a mind to do it," Mrs Harris chuckled, to Kate's annoyance. Mrs Harris was nice but she could be awfully stupid at times. Still, there was no-one else to talk to and Kate began to look forward to the trip to Silvermines. It would be more fun than doing messages for her mother and listening to Mrs Harris all day. She was glad when the evening came and it was time to go down to the theatre.

The place seemed different, with a small queue buying tickets in the foyer and people wandering around looking at the paintings and waiting for the doors to open. There was a buzz of excited talk from the wine bar, where every stool and chair was occupied and there was a continuous movement of people on the stairs leading to the basement snack-bar.

Sitting with her mother at the end of the fourth row, Kate found herself praying everything would go well so that they would all be in good humour the next day. Act 1 went smoothly enough, though there was a bit of coughing in the audience and only towards the end, when Chris carried in Chloe, lying limp and apparently lifeless in his arms, did Kate feel a little rustle of interest around her. Act 2 was certainly better than it had been the night before and Chris got through his drunk scene without hitch or hesitation, but a woman sitting behind Kate tittered when Chloe came on as the ghost. Kate, feeling her mother stiffen in the seat beside her, knew they could not relax yet.

But the minute the curtain went up on Jim Dolan, as the policeman in the trial scene, people started to laugh and, when he said: "I'm walking the world these twenty years and never met anything worse than myself," the curtain came down on an audience helpless with laughter. The applause was enthusiastic during the curtain calls and Maggie Masterson sighed with relief.

"It's comedy they're looking for," she told Kate. "We should have brought them one of Lady Gregory's farces, like *Hyacinth Halvey* or *Spreading the News* instead of this. Still, I think it will do business."

The cast was not sure whether to celebrate or not. There had been no disasters and Act 3 had saved the day and the play. They were all agreed about that. But only Jim Dolan, who was certainly never meant to be the star of the show, was really happy about the way everything had gone. Success or failure depended, Pat Masterson said, on the bookings for the rest of the week and that in turn would probably depend on what the papers said. They would just have to wait for the reviews.

But there was no *Limerick Leader* on a Tuesday, so the Mastersons had to set out for Silvermines without knowing whether the tour had started well or badly.

Everyone was still nervous and edgy so that even Bobby was glad of an outing and only made a token protest about being stuck with the girls. All the same, no-one felt much like talking as they drove out of Limerick along the main road towards Nenagh.

At the road junction just outside Birdhill, gardai were stopping all the cars, but they waved the Mastersons on after a quick glance into the empty boot. Kate kept her eyes fixed on the road ahead, searching for the crossing where they had been driven up on the ditch two days before. They had just passed a churchyard when they came to a lay-by like the one the car had turned out of, but it was different. It had little picnic tables like the ones where they had stopped for lunch and the road opposite ran gently downhill and not steeply. Surely she could not be so wrong in her memory of the place? And then suddenly there it was, just as she had pictured it, with the steep hill running down to Cappadine on the right and the two roads on the left, the second barely visible behind the lay-by. She gripped Bobby's arm and he nodded.

"That's where the car nearly hit us on Sunday," he said but Pat merely grunted something about Chris wanting to take better care in the future. A few miles further on, they swung right off the main road and, in less than ten minutes, were at the crossroads facing up the short broad village street leading to the church, backed by the steeply rising slope of Silvermines Mountain.

"There's Mary!" called Kate, as a small figure in jeans, with red pony-tail flying out behind, darted towards them.

Pat pulled up and Kate and Bobby scrambled out.

"Hi, Mary," Maggie said, before shouting after Bobby and Kate:

"We'll be back for you about half-three. Don't keep us waiting now!"

"They'll be here," Mary promised. "And there's no need to turn the car. You can take the Dolla Road there to Kilriffet."

"Right," Bobby said, as the car swung to its left and disappeared. "Where's this mine?"

"Come on," Mary answered, and set off towards the church.

"Will your father be there?" Kate asked, hurrying to keep up with her as she led the way up the road that curved around the church.

"Ah no," Mary said. "These are the old workings. He's at the open—cast mines opposite Moghul which is shut down now. That's back there," and she pointed to a road leading away from the church on their right.

"Why can't we go there?" Bobby wanted to know, but Mary looked at him as if he were crazy.

"You can't go where they're working and you can't get in to Moghul. Look, you can see the old mines up the mountains. Where the buildings are."

Kate looked up and saw three stone buildings like huge warehouses, jutting out from the side of the mountain ahead of them.

"What are they for?" she asked.

"Nothing now," Mary said. "They used to house the engines for pumping water out of the mines. You can still see some of the old machinery outside."

They climbed until even the top of the church spire was below them. They had left the road by now and were on the open mountainside. The ground under their feet had been flattened into a broad track that became several tracks, leading in different directions. Mary followed one that brought them to the first of the buildings. Now Kate could see it was really only a ruin, abandoned and lonely, with all the wood gone from it. Its floors and stairs were missing and only a rectangular opening showed where the door had once been. Bobby ran towards it but Mary called:

"You'd want to mind yourself in there. The roof's falling in."

Bobby looked irritated but he hesitated when he saw the stones that had already fallen from the crumbling roof.

"It's dark in there," he said.

"It was all lit up when we got home Sunday night," Mary told him.

Kate looked around but saw no sign of a lamp.

"How?" she asked.

"I don't know," Mary said, "but there was a light in the windows. I saw it. Dad said I imagined it, but I didn't."

"Didn't he see it then?" asked Bobby.

"No. It was only for a minute and by the time Dad looked it was dark again. He said it could have been the moon shining on the broken bits of glass in the windows."

Bobby took a few cautious steps into the building and looked up. He turned slowly in a circle, his eyes moving up and down the walls, with their three rows of windows, where the three floors had been. Then he looked at the ground.

"What are you doing?" asked Kate.

"Look at the windows!" instructed Bobby.

Kate peered up at the ones on the far side, but was afraid to go in far enough to see the others.

"What about them?"

"No glass," Bobby said. "Not even the smallest chip. The wind up here must be so strong it blew down even the bits clinging to the edge of the frames. And that must have happened a long time ago, so the broken bits were buried in the ground. There isn't a sliver of glass, only stones."

"It's muddy," Kate said. "I don't think it would take long for something sharp to get buried."

"But if there's no glass, what was the light I saw?" Mary wanted to know.

Bobby gave her an odd look. "What time did you see it?" he asked.

"When we got back from the theatre after your rehearsal," Mary said. "Around midnight."

"Look out!" cried Kate, as a lump of stone fell from the roof close to where Bobby was standing. "You'd better come out of there. That old place is dangerous!"

"And scary!" Bobby agreed as he joined the two girls outside. "I wouldn't like to come up here at night and I don't wonder you saw strange lights. I bet you anything you like this place is haunted!"

5

A Curlew's Cry

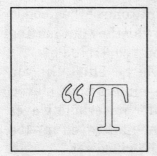here's many a man I heard say the same."

The voice came from close behind them and they all spun round, startled, to see a gaunt, elderly man whose white hair stood out around his bare head in an arc.

"Oh, Mr Mulcahy," Mary said, "you made me jump out of my skin!"

"Then this is no place for the likes of you," the man said, in the same soft voice that somehow made Kate feel uneasy. "For if a living man can put the heart across you, a dead one will surely still its beating for good."

"Are you saying the place is really haunted?" Kate asked. "I thought Bobby was just getting it up for us."

"Yeah, I was only messing," Bobby admitted.

"Maybe you were," Mr Mulcahy said, "but

there's many a true word spoken in jest. Mary here will know a lad met his death there a few years back."

"But that had nothing to do with ghosts!" Mary protested. "He fell into one of the flooded pits and drowned. That's why they put netting round the ones that weren't concreted over."

"Maybe he fell and maybe he didn't. Did you never hear tell how the miners that slaved down there in the dark for miserable wages were buried alive when a shaft caved in? It's said their spirits haunt the place yet."

Kate shivered. The sun that had shone on the dark green of the spruce and pine trees above the grassy banks of piled-up earth had disappeared behind the gathering clouds. Now there seemed to be something threatening about the grey skeletons of the buildings beside the deep scar left by the miners more than a century ago when they cut into the body of the green mountainside.

"They say that lad was tempted or driven over the edge of the pit-head," Mr Mulcahy continued. "And by no living man."

A wind shivered through the branches of the trees on the edge of the cut and Kate suddenly heard Chloe's voice saying: "Whenever you see a tree shaking there's a ghost in it." For the first time she felt that maybe it was true.

"I never heard that," Mary said, but she too looked uneasily at the trees and a shaft of sunlight which was pointing to the displaced soil like an accusing finger from a small tear in the dark cloud above.

"They might have kept it from you," Mr Mulcahy said, "for you were small enough at the time. But you'll not catch me up here late at night. There's many a thing I've seen from the road below, but I've kept my mouth shut. It doesn't do to be talking of these things."

"That's culchie talk," Bobby said scornfully.

"Is it now?" Mr Mulcahy looked at Bobby for a moment until Bobby looked away. "You young jackeens think you're smart, but there'll be more deaths before long, mark my words. That lump of stone that fell just now could have been meant as a warning."

"The only ghost I ever saw was on telly," Bobby retorted, annoyed with himself for giving way. "They're all like the one in our play: just people cod-acting with white powder on their faces!"

"All the same," Mr Mulcahy insisted, "I'd advise you to stay away from here if you don't want to get hurt. These old buildings are dangerous."

There was an awkward silence as if, Kate thought, Bobby and the old man were struggling with each other, though neither of them moved nor spoke. Then Mary interrupted the silent contest.

"We'd better go," she said.

"Come on then," Kate said, glad of the excuse.

For a moment Bobby hesitated. Then he followed the two girls along the track leading back towards the village.

"Who *is* that man?" Kate asked, as they reached the tarred road running up from the church.

"He lives over there," Mary said, nodding towards a modern two-storey house set back a little from the road and facing towards the mountains.

"He should have a good view of the mines from there," Bobby said. "If there were any ghosts on the go you'd think he'd be the first to spot them. What does he do all day?"

"He's a builder," Mary told him. "That's his pick-up truck pulled in off the road over there."

"He looks like a painting of a saint with a halo around his head," Kate said.

"Some saint!" Bobby snorted. "Wouldn't you think all the same he'd have more to do than running us? Why isn't he off somewhere building?"

"He's men working for him," Mary explained. "He doesn't always have to be there himself. You'd never know when he'd be home. I saw him heading off out the Dolla Road real late on Sunday night."

"Was that before or after you saw the mine building all lit up?" Bobby asked, suddenly interested.

"Oh, a fair bit later," Mary said. "I saw the light as I was getting out of the car, but I was just getting into bed when I heard the truck go by and saw it from the bedroom window."

"Maybe your man with the halo saw the light too!" Kate suggested.

"Sure to have," Bobby agreed, "if he was out and about soon afterwards."

"Maybe that's what he meant by the quare things he's seen that he doesn't talk about," Mary said.

"I dunno," Bobby said, "but I bet he doesn't really believe all that codology about ghosts. He just wanted to give us a scare."

"Why would he want to do that?" Kate asked.

"To get rid of us," Bobby said flatly. "He probably doesn't want us hanging around."

"We weren't doing him any harm," Kate

argued.

"He might be worried about his JCB," Mary suggested. "He keeps it in one of the buildings."

"So what?" Kate scoffed. "You can't nick a JCB!"

"There's some that would," Bobby grinned, "if they had to strip it down piece by piece. But maybe he was afraid we'd start messing with it."

Mary pushed open the door of a house in the middle of a street of small houses. At once, Kate caught the smell of turf smoke and the sound of a baby crying.

"Don't say anything about Mr Mulcahy," Mary whispered, pausing for a second in the open doorway. "She'll only give out to me." Then she led the way to the back of the house and into the kitchen.

Mrs Casey was bent over a pram with her back to them, but when she straightened Kate saw she had the same red hair as Mary.

"You're both very welcome," she said, smiling at Kate and Bobby. "I've a bit of cold ham and tomatoes ready for you. I'm afraid I couldn't manage anything hot."

"But ham's my favourite," Kate cried, glancing at the kitchen table, but there was nothing on it except a box of nappies.

"You can take your friends into the front parlour, Mary," her mother said. "I've had all I want and I didn't think they'd want to be bothered with the baby."

"He's sweet!" said Kate, holding out a finger for the baby to clutch in his little fist.

The baby threw his rattle out on to the floor and Kate stooped to pick it up.

"Come on," said Mary. "He'd have you at that all day," and she led them into the parlour where a meal was set out for them.

"Let's not take all day over it," said Bobby, his mouth full. "They'll be back for us in a couple of hours and I want to take another look around up there."

Kate looked at him uneasily. "I don't know if we ought to go back after what happened," she said.

"Of course we should!" Bobby retorted. "We didn't see a single mine yet, and I'm not letting old Halo-head stop us!"

"But if he's still around," Kate objected, "he'll only see us and run us again."

"Not if we keep out of sight of the house," Mary said. "We could go up the other way, by the old castle, keeping on the far side of the buildings and waste tips."

Kate had no wish to go back, whatever way

they went. The story about the boy that had drowned had given her the shakes. The gaunt skeletons of buildings and the scarred mountainside seemed haunted to her now. It was all very well for Bobby to say the talk about ghosts was all rubbish, but there was no getting away from the fact that people had died up there. The thought of all those miners, buried alive in one of the shafts, was horrible. Had they brought up the bodies or had one of the shafts become a tomb? If ghosts really went into trees, she thought, the trees along the cut would be the very place for them. But Bobby would only make a jeer of her if she said so. After all, seeing the mines had been her idea. If Mary was still willing to take them, how could she hold back?

So, when they had eaten their ham and tomatoes and several cuts of Mrs Casey's buttered soda bread, they thanked her politely and set off for the church once more. This time, though, they kept to the left of it, heading towards the square keep of the ruined castle. As they reached the top of the little hill where it stood, there was a loud shriek and Kate jumped back in fright. But it was only a pair of jackdaws, angry at being disturbed, who flew up from the ivy-covered tower.

It was not easy to see inside. You had to bend and peer up between the crumbling stones and Kate was fearful at what they might see, but there was nothing but grass and weeds, where once a wooden floor had been.

"Come on," Bobby said. "There's nothing here," and they set off again up the track.

"What's that building over there?" Kate asked Mary, pointing to the remains of high walls beyond them over to the left.

"Another engine house maybe. Or they could have used it for roasting the zinc oxide," Mary replied. "I doubt if anyone knows now. These mines haven't been worked for over a hundred years."

"There's a lake on the other side of it," Bobby said.

"It's not really a lake," Mary corrected him. "It's a flooded mine. An open cast one like the one where my Da works, but there's nothing to see there either."

The track they were on climbed to join another, leading up from the flooded mine to the grey stone buildings where they had been before lunch. As they reached this second track, damp from the heavy weekend rains, Kate saw it was deeply marked by car tracks, the treads of the tyres clearly etched into the red-brown earth.

"There's been a car along here," she said. "Look! It went down to the flooded mine."

"Funny place to take a car," Bobby commented. "There must be something down there after all," and he turned left along the new track, walking on the shoulder between the tyre ruts.

Mary and Kate followed him to the lip of the mine. The mine itself was huge, stretching away into the distance almost to where the forest road climbed the slope beyond. Inside the rim, the ground fell away steeply to the surface of the lake, formed by the rain water that covered the bottom of the mine. Then Kate noticed something odd. The tyre tracks continued right to the water's edge.

"They drove right in!" she gasped in horror, her mind already on drowning, but Bobby only laughed.

"Pushed it, more likely," he said. "Someone was getting rid of an old banger, that's all!"

They turned and went back up the hill towards the mine buildings. Half-way up, the track branched out into a tangle of tracks, running in all directions.

"They all go to different mine shafts," Mary explained. "Come and see."

They followed each path in turn, only to find that every one ended in the centre of encircling mounds of earth, dug out of the mines. In the very middle of each of these little grassy clearings was a mineshaft, surrounded by wire netting. They walked round the netting, but it was impossible to see down into the shafts.

"Is that all?" Bobby asked, disappointed.

"Ah no," Mary said. "There's dozens more, but they're all much the same. I told you there was nothing to see."

"Then let's forget about them," Kate said quickly. She experienced the same prickly feeling she had felt between her shoulder blades when she had heard the story of the boy that drowned. It was an odd sort of feeling, as if someone she could not see was watching her.

"Let's have a look at your man's JCB," Bobby suggested. So they went on up towards the buildings, taking care to keep out of sight of the road.

When they reached the buildings, they found that part of the ground in front of the nearer ones had been covered in concrete, to form a level platform and, at one end of this, was the remains of ancient machinery.

"What was that for?" Bobby asked, inspecting a section of narrow gauge rail track and a broken pulley.

"Hauling the trucks," Mary said. "They brought the ore here for crushing to separate it from the rock."

The end wall of the building she pointed to had partly collapsed, giving it the appearance of an ancient aeroplane hanger but, instead of a plane, it housed a yellow JCB.

"He's had it out," Kate said. "Look at the tracks!"

Bobby inspected the wheel marks, running from inside the building and disappearing as they reached the concrete platform. Then he shook his head.

"Those aren't JCB tracks," he said. "They're smaller and they don't have the thick treads. There must have been something else parked beside it."

"Maybe it was the car they dumped in the flooded mine," Kate suggested.

Bobby crossed the concrete platform to the point where the wheel marks appeared again on the far side. They led on uphill towards the road by a track parallel to the one they had followed that morning. He shook his head.

"It went the other way," he pointed out.

"Maybe it was the pick-up truck," Mary volunteered.

"Now you're talking!" Bobby grabbed her by the arm in his excitement. "When you saw the truck on Sunday night it could have been coming from up here!"

"Then where did the old banger come from?" Kate asked, surprised at Bobby's sudden interest.

"That's what we've got to find out," Bobby told her. "And maybe it wasn't a banger after all. We must go back and pick up the tracks."

"We don't need to go all the way back," Kate protested. She wanted to give up all this stupid detective nonsense and get away from this place, that gave her such a sense of unease. "Can't we find the tracks from up here? They must come up somewhere."

Bobby shook his head obstinately.

"We've got to make sure they're the right tracks. There seems to have been a lot of traffic around here lately."

"Does it really matter?" Kate asked. After all, it was really none of their business what a builder did with his own JCB and pick-up truck.

"It might," Bobby said. "It might matter a lot. Supposing you'd nicked a car and used it for a robbery. You'd know people would be looking for it, so you'd want to get rid of it, wouldn't you? You might drive it up here, dump it in a flooded mine and have another car — or a truck, maybe — ready for you to change into."

"Just because you know there was a robbery," Kate scoffed. "Why should the robbers come all the way up here?"

"Because it's the sort of place no-one would look," Bobby answered, "and the buildings would be great for hiding a get-away car."

It was like something you'd see on telly, Kate thought, and Bobby was having a great time playing who-dunnits. It was all nonsense, of course. But just suppose it wasn't? If it were true, there would be more than ghosts to worry about. Who could tell what robbers might do to stop people uncovering their trail?

"I bet you that's what the light was that Mary saw," Bobby went on.

"What?"

"Them switching on the truck lights inside the building."

"But they were only on for a second," Mary objected.

"They didn't want to be seen," Bobby said. "The driver maybe switched them on and someone shouted at him to put them off again." Suddenly something struck him. "Hey! We were talking about Mary seeing the lights when old Halo-head appeared this morning. He could have heard us. No wonder he wanted to run us if he did!"

It was getting worse and worse, Kate thought.

"That's maybe not why at all!" she said, trying to discourage him.

"Maybe not," Bobby agreed, "but I'm going to find out!" And before Kate could do anything more to stop him he ran off down the track in the direction of the flooded mine.

"Will we go with him?" Mary asked, hesitating between the two of them.

"Let's try and find where the wheel marks come up," Kate suggested. "There can't be that many tracks the car could have used."

It would be quicker than going all the way back down again, she thought, and the sooner she could get the whole thing over and done with, the better. Once Bobby found the tracks he might realise they led nowhere and go back down to the village.

The two girls strolled across the concrete platform onto a stretch of flattened grass beyond. Suddenly Kate stopped. Her foot had struck something hard. Looking down, she saw a circle of concrete in the ground, like an unusually large manhole.

"What's that?" she asked.

"Just another mineshaft," Mary told her. "One of the ones that's concreted in."

"There's letters cut into it," Kate said, stooping to read them.

"Only the name of the pit," Mary explained. "They always mark them like that when they seal them."

"There's another!"

As she moved from one sealed shaft to another, Kate tried to picture them before they were sealed. The men down below would have been blasting the rock face, so that the lumps of rock would fall down the shaft into the horizontal passage below. Then they would have been hauled to the surface and trundled along the little railway line in trucks. The place that was now so quiet would have echoed to the sound of blasting and warning shouts. And then one of them had caved in. Which one was it, she wondered. Which had suddenly changed from a mineshaft into a living tomb?

She was startled out of her thoughts by a sudden cry.

"What was that?" she asked Mary sharply.

"A curlew, maybe."

"I thought someone cried out!"

"Curlews sound like that. It's a lonesome cry

they make."

Beyond the mineshafts was another track and they saw the wheel marks right away.

"I knew there was no need to go back!" Kate cried. "Wait till we tell Bobby!"

They went a short way down the track until they could see across to the flooded mine below, but there was no sign of Bobby. They called his name, softly at first because they did not want to attract attention, then louder. There was no reply.

"He's messing again," Kate said. "Just to make me go all the way down because I said I didn't want to. I bet he's hiding behind one of the waste tips."

But she only said it to avoid facing her fears. She had been afraid all afternoon that something unpleasant would happen. Now she could only cling to a desperate hope that it had not already happened.

They went all the way down, searching the waste tips as they went. They looked into the ruined castle and even went right to the lip of the flooded mine, but Bobby was nowhere to be seen.

6
A Chance to Fly

ate was getting really worried now.

"What's Bobby playing at?" she muttered. "They'll be back for us soon and there'll be ructions if we're not ready and waiting."

"Maybe he went looking for us," Mary suggested. "He might have gone up one track while we came down the other."

"He must have heard us calling him," Kate said.

"Well, he's not here."

Mary looked along the lip of the mine to the point where the tyre tracks led down to the water's edge. That was where Bobby had been going, to pick up the trail and follow it.

"He would have gone up that way," she said. Then she froze. "Look at the footmarks!"

Kate ran over to the tracks and then she

laughed.

"We made them ourselves," she said, fitting her right foot into the print she had left in the muddy soil.

"Not those. These!"

Then Kate saw the other, larger footmarks. They had the heavy imprint of a man's boot.

"Were they there before?" she whispered.

Mary shook her head.

"They were not," she said. "There were no prints there then. Just the tyre marks. Someone else has been here since."

Kate shivered. Was it the owner of the boots she had felt watching them? And had he been here at the same time as Bobby, while they were looking at the concrete-lidded mines?

"Come on!" Kate said.

They followed the footsteps over the lip of the mine and across the rough, sloping ground leading to the water's edge. Suddenly Kate clutched Mary's arm and pointed to where the tracks met up with a set of smaller prints.

"Those are Bobby's," Kate said. "I'm sure of it. Oh, let's hurry!"

The two sets of prints circled the side of the mine, under the lip. Suddenly, Kate stopped dead, grabbing Mary's arm.

"Look out!" she cried.

They had almost fallen into a pit right in front of them, half-hidden by an overhanging gorse bush. The miners had dug deeper here, cutting into the side of the slope leading up from the larger workings. Then they heard a faint moan.

Holding on to the roots of the bush, where they were partly exposed at the edge of the pit, Kate peered over. At the bottom lay Bobby, face downwards, one leg tucked beneath him.

"Bobby!" Kate cried, torn between relief at finding him and fear at the stillness of his crumpled body. "Are you all right?"

When he answered her he spoke in a strained voice, partly muffled by his position.

"I can't move," he said. "I think my ankle's broken."

Still holding on to the wiry roots of the bush, Kate began to lower herself cautiously into the pit. Suddenly the soil crumbled beneath her, the roots tore away from her grasp and she fell the last few feet, landing beside Bobby at the bottom of the pit. Thankful she had not fallen on top of him, she slid one arm gently under his body, but the minute she attempted to raise him from the ground he let out a yell and fell back again, wincing with pain.

"It's no good," she called up to Mary, whose

head she could just see peering over the edge. "You'll have to get help. I'll stay here with him."

Mary nodded so that her pony-tail swung.

"I'll be as quick as I can," she called back. Then her head disappeared.

"I didn't fall," Bobby insisted. "I was pushed!"

Kate caught her breath. So she had not been worrying needlessly.

"Who by?" she asked.

"I couldn't see!" Bobby spoke in a series of little efforts, his teeth clenched with pain. "I followed the car tracks down to the water. I wanted to see the car. To be able to identify it. In case it was stolen. But I couldn't see a thing. I thought I could see better from the other side. The light was better over there. And the water wasn't rippling so much. There was an overhanging rock. I was going towards it. Then I was charged from above. I never heard whoever it was coming."

"You should have screamed for us."

"I did! As I fell. There was an awful pain. Then everything went black."

"You must have fainted," Kate said. "That's why you didn't hear us calling you. But why didn't we hear you?" Then she remembered.

"Or maybe we did. I heard something but Mary thought it was a curlew."

Then something else struck her. "He could have pushed you into the water!" she gasped. "You would have drowned!"

"Maybe he meant to. He pushed me hard enough to. Only the pit was in the way!"

"Maybe he didn't see it!" Kate said.

"Maybe not. I didn't. I suppose it was because I was looking at the water."

"I think the gorse bush hid it," Kate told him. She drew her breath in sharply. "D'you really think he meant to drown you?"

"Why not? He drowned the other boy, didn't he?"

"What?"

"Don't you remember? Old Halo-head told us about it. He even said he was supposed to have been pushed."

"He said 'by no living man'," Kate reminded him. "I don't think it was a ghost pushed you."

"It felt more like a charging bull! But I think that's what that ghost is: a load of bull. I think something's been going on here — for years maybe. That other boy might have been on to them. So they got rid of him. And then we started sniffing around. Now they want to get rid of us too!"

Kate shivered. The man might come back. His footprints had gone on, up over the lip of the mine. But he could always come back. She hoped Mary would hurry. Then she remembered something else.

"Bobby," she said, "what about the show tonight? You won't be able to play!"

"I know!" Bobby groaned. "Pat's going to kill me!"

Suddenly Kate knew exactly what the solution was. The only problem was how to get everyone else to agree.

"Not if we have it all planned," she said.

"There's nothing to plan," Bobby told her miserably. "He'll have to find someone else, some Limerick boy."

"No, he won't," Kate said firmly. "I'll do it!"

"You can't!"

"Why not? I've seen you do it lots of times."

"You're a girl!"

"The audience won't know that. I'll wear your costume."

"It's too big for you."

"Only a little. I'll tuck the trousers up a little. And I can push my hair up under the cap. I'll play him a bit younger."

"D'you know the lines?"

"Of course."

"What's the cue?"

"When Chloe says: 'We must have leave to do that!' Then you run in through the door and go to down left of Chris."

"Say the lines," Bobby ordered. "Say them as if you were me!"

Kate took a deep breath. She had never thought her first audition would be done for Bobby and in a place like this.

"Well, go on then!"

She pictured herself, left in charge of the racing stables, getting worried and hurrying for help.

"The horses are getting uneasy in the stable," she said. "Will you come and quiet them down?"

There was a pause. Kate realised she was almost as worried about what Bobby would say as she was that the owner of the boots might come back.

"You'll be O.K.," Bobby said, and Kate wondered if the effort it seemed to take for him to say it was only because of the pain in his ankle.

She gave his shoulder a gentle squeeze.

"Thanks, Bobby," she said. "Maybe it will only be for tonight."

She heard the sound of men's voices and Mr

Casey's head appeared over the top of the pit. It was the second time, she thought, that he had come to their rescue. Then she realised it must be getting late if he had finished his shift at the mines.

"Well, we'll want you out of the way for a start," he called down to Kate. "Catch hold of this," and the end of a rope dropped down beside her. She began to climb it, as she had often climbed ropes in the gym, but she had hardly pulled herself up more than an inch or two when the rope was hauled up with her clinging to it. Hands pulled her clear of the pit and she saw that they belonged to two men with Mr Casey.

"Go on back to the cross with Mary," Mr Casey said, picking up a length of plank. "We don't want your parents hunting the village for you. We won't be long after you."

"It hurts Bobby to move," she began but Mr Casey cut her short.

"Leave it to us," he said. "We've brought up more injured men out of pits than you've had hot dinners."

Mary and Kate hurried down to the cross but there was no car waiting. Kate was glad because, for all her brave talk, she was dreading what her father would say. While they stood waiting Mary noticed Kate's anxious face.

"Will they be mad at you?" she asked.

Before Kate could answer she saw the black Audi coming towards them. She also saw the men coming down the side of the hill towards the church. Two of them held a plank between them like a stretcher and on the plank lay Bobby.

Her mother leaned back in the passenger seat and opened the back door of the car.

"Get in," she said. "Where's Bobby?"

Then she looked to see what Kate was watching so closely and gave a little cry.

"He's all right," Kate said quickly. "Honestly! I was with him. It's only his ankle."

"Is that all?" her father asked with heavy sarcasm. "And are they going to carry him on stage like that tonight?"

"That's all settled," Kate said in a rush, before her nerve went altogether. "Bobby says I can play his part."

"Did he now?" Pat Masterson was icy with anger. "So he's the producer of the show now, is he?"

"But I know the cue and the lines," Kate said. "I said them for him and he thought I'd be O.K. And I can wear his clothes if I roll up his trousers!"

"Maybe the two of you would like to take over the running of the company," her father began, the awful note of irony still in his voice, but Maggie interrupted.

"Oh, for heaven's sake, it's only two lines. Who's going to notice what she's like? But if Bobby's broken something I don't know what we'll do with him for the rest of the tour. I might have known it was a mistake to bring them with us."

She jumped out of the car and ran to meet the little procession, just as it reached the main street.

"He's fine, Missus," Mr Casey reassured her. "I wouldn't say he was too bad at all. We brought him down this way just to be on the safe side, like."

"Oh Bobby, you clown," Maggie said, half-worried, half-angry. "How are we going to get you into the car like that?"

"The mine doctor lives just across the road," Mr Casey said. "Wouldn't it be best to let him take a look?"

"Oh yes, that would be much better than waiting to get him to hospital," Maggie agreed, looking relieved. So she and the little procession went across to the house with the brass plate on it.

When they came out again, Bobby was walking, or rather half-hopping, with Mr Casey supporting him.

"There's nothing broken, thank God," Maggie told Pat cheerfully. "It's a bad sprain, the doctor says, but he's strapped it up and he'll be right as rain in a week or so, if he rests it."

"Get him into the car then," Pat said, impatient to be off.

"He's not coming," Maggie said. "I've agreed to leave him here for a few days. Mr Casey very kindly offered to have him and it makes life a lot easier. We really can't expect Mrs Harris to look after him when he's got to keep the leg up as much as possible. And the doctor will be able to take another look at the ankle on Friday."

Kate ran over to Bobby.

"It's only for one week and Mary will keep you company," she whispered, "and while you're here you can be keeping your eyes and ears open for clues."

"You bet!" Bobby gave a grin to hide his disappointment. "And if you need any help with the part ask Chris. Just do it like you did for me and you'll be fine!"

Sitting by herself on the back seat of the Audi as they drove towards Limerick, Kate was not so sure. Until that moment, all she had thought about was persuading everyone to let her play the part. That had been easier than she had dared to hope. Now that that obstacle was out of the way, it suddenly dawned on her that in a few hours she would be going on stage for the very first time in her father's company, and without any proper rehearsal. Her mother had said no-one would notice if she was bad, but that was no comfort. She wanted to be good. Most of all, she wanted her father to think she was good and to tell her so. And for that, she thought, she was going to need all the luck in the world.

7

More than Meets the Eye

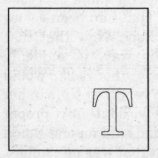

The minute she got to the theatre, Kate hurried to tell Chris what had happened.

"Didn't I tell you your chance would come?" he grinned. "It just came sooner than I thought."

"I only hope I'm able for it," Kate said, suddenly feeling sick.

"Patience and perseverance will drive a snail to Jerusalem," Chris told her. "We'll go over it on stage, just the two of us, until we know you *are* able for it. We'd best go now, before they let the house in."

"Oh thanks, Chris. Are you sure you have the time?"

"You must always make time to edge the tool if the job's to be done right," Chris said. "Come on!"

They ran through the short passage three or four times, with Chris speaking Chloe's lines.

"That's enough," he said, "and enough is as good as a feast. I have to get going. Slip on Bugsy's things till we see how you look."

Kate put on the stableboy's costume, jammed the cap on her head and went to show herself to Chris. He turned from the dressing-room mirror and whistled.

"Bugsy the Second," he said. "You're the dead spit of your brother like that. You'll want to darken your skin a bit, though. Here," and he handed her a tube of make-up. "Rub this over your face and neck and blend it well at the edges so you don't get a line."

When she had that done he looked at her critically. "I'll just thicken your brows a bit. Turn to the light." He gave her brows a few quick strokes with a brown eye pencil and seemed satisfied. "That's grand now. You'll do."

Jim stuck his head in the door and called "Beginners, please!" Like Kate, he would not be needed on stage until the last act, but he had plenty to do backstage, making sure everything and everyone was ready.

"And we want no second night downer," he added. "The critic from the *Leader's* in tonight."

Chris made a face.

"I hate having the press in on the second night," he said.

"It's my first night," Kate told him.

"So it is, Bugsy — so it is." Chris seemed to have given her the name along with the costume and, in a strange way, Kate was glad.

"Here's luck to us both!" Chris added, as he followed Jim down the stairs to the stage. Kate came behind them, creeping into the wings to watch. Watching the others took her mind off her own nerves.

She knew second night performances were often flat, after the excitement of an opening night, but she felt that the first two acts went well, even better than yesterday. As they began changing the set for the third act, she slipped back to the dressing-room with the others, for a last check on her costume and make-up. Looking into the mirror, she saw Bobby's face staring back at her. She felt that he silently wished her luck, and was sorry for him, being out of the show after only one performance. Then she forgot about him. It was her own stomach, not his, that suddenly seemed as full of flutterings as a bush of purple buddleia covered in butterflies.

"Good luck, Kate!" whispered the ghostly Chloe, as she slipped silently past her on to the stage. Seconds later Kate heard her speak the cue. As she ran on stage to say her two lines, something odd happened. Suddenly she found herself thinking, not of being left alone in charge of a thoroughbred horse on whose win everyone's hopes hung, but of Bobby. It had been madness to leave him in Silvermines, where perhaps someone had already tried to kill him. And although the lines she spoke were those in the play, asking Lawrence Scarry to come with her to quieten the horses, in her mind she was pleading with Chris to come with her to make sure that Bobby was all right. Then it was all over and she was back in the wings again, her heart thudding.

Another few minutes and she heard again the laugh that swept the audience as Jim spoke the final line. Then Chris was beside her, pulling her into the line-up on stage for the curtain call.

"Come on, Bugsy," he said. "You deserve it."

With the others, she bowed, as she had so often watched her father bow, twice, three times, and then the curtain stayed closed. Her father turned from his place in the centre of the stage beside Chloe and smiled at her.

"Not bad at all, Kate," he said. "We'll make an actress of you yet!"

Kate flushed. To anyone who did not know her father it might not sound much, but she knew that for him it was the height of praise. The rest of the cast said kind words to her also, but it was the grin Chris gave her that pleased her most.

"You were a real help, Bugsy," he said. "You seemed so bothered about the old horse that you had me real upset I wasn't let go to see to him! If you were a year or two older I'd take you across to Gleesons and buy you a drink for that!"

Kate would have given anything to go too. It would have made her feel one with the rest of the cast, to go with them to relax after the show. She knew that everyone was always too strung up to go straight home and that it was the need to unwind gradually in company, not the drink, that made them rush to change so as to get to the pub before closing time. But Maggie would not hear of it.

"You did very well," she said in her brisk, business-like manner, "but we've had quite enough excitement for one day. Besides you're under age and the guards might not be too easily convinced that you had nothing stronger in your coke!"

"But everyone always goes for a drink after their first performance," Kate pleaded.

"Not at twelve," Maggie said firmly. "It's bad enough that our original stableboy has a sprained ankle, without having his understudy suffering from a hangover from the smell of the cork. You've to play tomorrow night too, you know, so try to get a good night's sleep."

Kate never felt less like sleeping. She was far too worked up, but her legs ached from scrambling up and down over all the waste tips and the worry and excitement had left her really tired. She lay in bed, going over and over in her mind everything that had happened. Then she thought about Bobby, in bed at the Caseys, and wondered if he was able to sleep. Maybe the baby cried at night, she thought. She tried to picture the inside of the little house and fell asleep wondering where they had found room for Bobby.

*   *   *

Mrs Casey had taken Bobby's appearance, hopping in the door on the arm of her husband, a lot more calmly than his own mother would have done, Bobby thought, as he lay looking up at the kitchen ceiling and wishing his ankle would stop throbbing.

"Get the blankets out of the press, Mary," she had said, "and put them near the cooker to air. "I hope," she had continued, turning to Bobby, "you'll not mind sleeping in here. It will be like the times I stayed with my grandparents and they put me to sleep on the old settle bed in the kitchen. And it will save you climbing the stairs with the bad foot."

Bobby had lain awake a long time, listening to the silence but, in the end, he had fallen asleep.

Next day, he woke early, just as he had always done when they stayed with Aunt Delia, disturbed by the unfamiliar sounds of the country. Instead of the hum of early morning traffic moving along the canal, he could hear cattle lowing and the crowing of cocks. Then the baby upstairs began to crow too and soon the whole house was stirring, for Mr Casey was still on the early shift at the mines. Bobby, his mind racing now to make sense of all that had happened the day before, was anxious to talk to Mary when no-one else was around, for he had decided to say nothing that might alarm her parents.

As soon as they were alone, he told her everything that he had told Kate while he lay at the bottom of the pit. Mary's eyes opened wide.

"Are you saying 'twas Mr Mulcahy pushed you?" she asked in disbelief.

"I don't know who pushed me," Bobby said. "It felt like Superman and I don't see old Halo-head in the role. But he's in on it all some way. I'm sure of it. And I'm more and more certain it's to do with the robbery over at Ballina. I mean, it was the night of the robbery you saw the lights and his pick-up truck and everything."

"Kate thought that car that put you up on the ditch was in it too," Mary said.

"I know, but the timing's all wrong. The robbery didn't happen till much later."

"I was thinking about that," Mary said slowly. "You know your show that I saw Sunday night?"

"What about it?"

"Well, you were only practising, weren't you?"

"Rehearsing," Bobby corrected her. "It was the final rehearsal. We call it the dress rehearsal, because we're dressed for the performance and have the make-up and proper lighting and everything."

"Well, I was thinking," Mary went on. "You have to do that before you do the show in front of an audience."

"Of course," Bobby said.

"So maybe robbers do the same. Try it out, like, to make sure nothing goes wrong."

"You can't try out a robbery," Bobby scoffed. "D'you think they march into a house they're going to rob and say: don't mind me, I'm only rehearsing?"

"But they might try out the get-away and things like that," Mary suggested, "to see how long it took them and that."

"The watch!" Bobby yelled in excitement. "Kate said the man in the car looked at his watch as they shot across the road." Then he shook his head. "But it still won't wash. They were on the wrong road. I checked the signposts yesterday on the way here. There's a much quicker way to get from Ballina and a get-away car's going to take the quickest road."

"They might not," Mary challenged.

"Of course they would, stupid. If you nicked something and you knew the fuzz would be coming after you, you wouldn't go miles out of your way, would you?"

"Sarsfield did," Mary said, "and he only had a horse."

"Now what are you on about?" Bobby demanded impatiently.

"When General Sarsfield rode from Limerick to stop King Billy's guns taking the city in 1690, he rode miles out of his way."

And country people went miles out of the way to solve a problem, Bobby thought. But dragging the Siege of Limerick into it was going too far altogether.

"I suppose you learned all that in school," he said in a superior sort of way.

"Everyone here knows that," Mary said, "because it all happened just here. Sarsfield rode through Bushfield Cross and forded the Mulkear River near Aughmheara. That's less than four miles from here. The tourist board have signposts up now, showing the way he went. He rode north from Limerick beyond Ballina and then east as far as here, though he was going to Ballyneety and that's south of Limerick. He rode almost in a circle. And he travelled 65 miles, though Ballyneety's less than 20 miles from Limerick."

"He sounds a bit of a nutter," Bobby muttered, trying to remember what he'd learned about Sarsfield's ride.

"He was very clever," Mary insisted. "He knew the king's men were out to get him, so he went all the ways they didn't expect. The robbers might have done that too."

"Avoiding the places the guards might set up road blocks," Bobby said slowly. "And they had them all over the place. We were stopped twice. But they hadn't one where the old road comes out at the lay-by."

"Maybe they learned about Sarsfield too," Mary said, and Billy thought that he had been wrong about country people. Maybe like Sarsfield, if they took a roundabout way of getting where they were going it got them further in the end.

"It fits!" he cried. "It all fits! We'd better get going."

"You can't go anywhere," Mary pointed out. "You're supposed to be resting your ankle."

"Yeah, and that's a lucky break, or I wouldn't be here," Bobby said.

"You mean, a lucky sprain," Mary giggled. "But what can we do? We can't go to the guards. They'd only laugh at us. It's all just supposing."

"That's why I was trying to get a look at the car in the flooded mine," Bobby said. "If we had a description of that at least there'd be something to go on."

"You said you were only going down to pick up the tyre tracks."

"I was. Then I thought it would be even better if I could get a gawk at the car itself. Now I can't even follow the track up from the quarry."

"There's no need," Mary told him. "Kate and I found where it comes up. That's why we were looking for you — to tell you that. They come up on to the far track opposite the buildings."

"And then where do they go?"

"We never found out. We went looking for you."

"Then we must find out now, before someone muddies the trail. If old Halo-head thought we were following them he could drive his pick-up truck all over them till there were tyre marks going every whichway."

"*You* can't follow anything," Mary said. "You can't even walk!"

"All I need is a crutch," Bobby said. "Like Long John Silver in *Treasure Island*. It's road all the way up the hill and the track's not bad going."

"It must have been a good dirt road when those mines were worked," Mary agreed. "But if we went by the road we'd have to pass right by Mulcahy's."

"Is there anywhere we can spy on the house without being seen?"

"You can see everything for miles around from the top of the church tower," Mary said.

"Brill," Bobby said. "Then we can wait till he goes out and nip up before he comes back."

"You'd never get up the tower even with a crutch," Mary pointed out.

"Can't you go up and keep a look out while I wait in the church? Now, all we need is a crutch. Have you anything in the house that would do?"

Mary shook her head.

"Unless you used my Dad's hurley — you know, upside down under your armpit."

"The very thing. Can you get it?"

"He'll kill me if he finds out."

"So don't tell him! Oh, go on! I'll take care of it, honest!"

That was how, half-an-hour later, Bobby came to be sitting at the end of the pew nearest to the door of the empty church. Mr Casey's hurley was hidden under the seat while Bobby kept an eye on the door, ready to appear deep in prayer the minute he heard it creak open. He waited for a long time before Mary appeared.

"He's away," she whispered excitedly. "He headed out the Dolla Road in the truck. You wouldn't know how long he'd be gone, though. We'd best hurry."

Bobby pulled the hurley from under the pew, tucked it under his armpit and hobbled out after her. He was awkward with it at first and the long uphill climb left him exhausted. But by the time they were well down the gentle sloping track which led to the buildings, he was using his makeshift crutch like a vaulting pole, swinging himself along so fast that Mary could hardly keep up with him. Fear that the trail might have been spoiled spurred him on ever faster. But when Mary led him away from the buildings to the far track and he saw the wheel marks clearly etched in the soil he nearly shouted with triumph.

"Where does this track go?"

"It can't go far," she told him. "There's a big cut up ahead."

They followed the wheel marks along the track, which at first ran back up the hill they had just come down, on a path closer to the slope of the mountain. Then it swung to the left towards the rock face, and began to descend between two high banks.

"Waste tips," Mary said. "There must be more mines in here."

"There are," Bobby agreed. "I can see wire netting."

Suddenly the track became the stem of a T-junction running past wire netting enclosures on both sides. The car tracks turned right, and Bobby followed them. After passing two netting-enclosed mineshafts, the track began to climb steeply. Bobby found it harder going and the pressure of the hurley under his arm was beginning to be painful. Then a last steep scramble brought them out onto a dirt track.

"The quarry road," Mary said. "It runs from the quarry down to the road we came on. The track to the buildings comes out onto it lower down. We're back where we started."

"And the tracks turn right onto it too," Bobby groaned in disappointment. "They drove up from the road, down this track and into the quarry. We did all that for nothing."

"Only for one thing," Mary began and then stopped.

Bobby sat down on the side of the ditch and rested the hurley beside him. He knew by now that Mary was thinking things out and that it might take her some time. But he also knew by now that her thoughts might be worth waiting for.

"Well?" he asked encouragingly.

"Well, I was thinking," Mary began slowly. "If they only wanted to ditch the car, why didn't they take the main track past the buildings? It's not nearly as bumpy or steep as this one. And they would have had to pass the other one to get here. Why would they drive on past the turn and take this track?"

"So they wouldn't be seen?" suggested Bobby. "This track is hidden by the waste tips."

"But they'd still be seen coming up the quarry road," Mary said, "and on the lower track they'd be hidden by the buildings in a matter of seconds."

"So you tell me why?"

"Well, I was thinking," Mary said again, "I was thinking maybe they stopped somewhere up here on the way."

"Where?"

"I don't know."

"And why?"

"To let someone in or out? Or something, maybe?"

Bobby gasped. It was beginning to make sense. "The stolen picture would have been in the car," he said. "They would have had to stop somewhere to take it out before they dumped the car, wouldn't they?"

"But why take it out here? The truck was in the mine building. If they wanted to transfer the picture into that they'd have driven to the buildings."

"*If* they wanted to. But suppose they were hiding it here?"

"But there's nowhere up here to hide it."

"Except," Bobby said slowly, "in one of the mineshafts."

"Sure they're all flooded," Mary argued. "Every bit of rain water drains down into them. You couldn't keep anything in them that wouldn't be destroyed!"

Bobby knew she was right. Even if the mines were not flooded, they would be no place to keep a valuable painting. He remembered the man from the National Gallery during a school tour telling them how the paint flaked off old paintings unless they were kept at the right temperature and everything. But he hated to admit he had been wrong.

"Maybe they had some way of doing it," he said. "I'm going to look anyway."

He picked up the hurley and levered himself to his feet. He was tired now and knew he was only wasting time, but he propelled himself back down the slope to the first mineshaft. It was exactly the same as the ones they had looked at the day before: a hole with netting all round it and no way of getting near it even to look down into it. And the other one would be the same. There was no point in hobbling on further since movement was becoming more and more painful. He started to turn back and then he heard Mary cry out. While he had been circling the first mineshaft, she had gone on to the second.

"Come and look at this!" she called.

He hobbled over as fast as he could, but saw only a mineshaft like the one he had just inspected. Then he saw what Mary was looking at. In the netting on the far side, someone had cut a big round hole.

8

Never Say Die

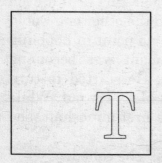hat morning Kate woke late and Chris was already at his breakfast when she reached the dining-room.

"Well, Bugsy," he said, "how does it feel to be a star?"

"You mustn't laugh at me," she said, remembering how the whole company had begun calling Bobby "Bugsy" for thinking himself a star after playing only one small part in the Olympia.

"You did very well, all the same," Chris said. "It's scary enough having to go on for someone else like that. It happened to me one time in Tralee and I wasn't the better of it for days. You've a right to feel pleased with yourself this morning."

But Kate felt anything but pleased with herself. What had possessed her to ask Bobby to keep an eye on the robbers? She had wanted to comfort him for losing his part in the play, to make him feel important. But she had only encouraged him to add to the danger he was in.

Bobby never gave up on anything, once he had made a start and now she had prompted him to stay with it. He would go back up to the quarry despite his sprained ankle and whoever had tried to kill him would try again. And whoever it was was no amateur. The newspaper had said the robbers were thought to be professional criminals. They might have failed to kill him the first time, but they would not make the same mistake twice.

That fear had been in her mind as she woke and, as she dressed, it had increased. She would have to get back to Silvermines somehow and make sure Bobby did nothing foolish.

"Chris," she said, "Would you do something for me?"

"Anything, Bugsy," he grinned. "Just think of it as the drink I would have liked to buy you last night!"

"Then will you run me over to Silvermines this morning? I wouldn't ask you if I could get a bus, but they only run on Saturdays."

"Ah, Bugsy, I don't want to lose a second stableboy. That place seems a bit hard on the ankles!"

"Please, Chris," Kate begged. "It's important. There's no way Maggie would take me again after yesterday and I'm worried about Bobby."

"He's in good hands, Bugsy. Mr Casey struck me as a man you could put your trust in."

"You don't understand," Kate pleaded. "I think Bobby's in danger." And she told Chris everything that had happened from the moment they had met Mr Mulcahy up at the mine building to her last whispered parting with Bobby.

"So you see," she ended, "I must go out there today or they'll kill him. I know they will!"

"Are you sure you're not seeing a mountain where there's only a molehill?" Chris asked. "The car tracks could have been there for days and there's many a person gets rid of old clapped-out cars."

"Bobby's ankle's real enough, isn't it?" Kate demanded. "You know it must be bad if it's stopped him playing in the show."

"I won't argue with you over that, Bugsy," Chris agreed, "but he could have fallen into the pit without being pushed."

"Then why should he say he was pushed?"

"So your father wouldn't give out to him for missing the show through his own carelessness, maybe. Let's face it, Bugsy, no-one saw it happen and you told me even he couldn't say who it was that did it."

"So why did Mr Mulcahy take his truck out around midnight on Sunday, after Mary had seen the light up at the mines?"

"I don't doubt he could give you a good reason. As for the light, no-one but Mary saw it and even she couldn't be sure what it was."

"You don't believe a word I'm saying," cried Kate, near to tears.

"Indeed and I do, Bugsy," Chris assured her. "There's no-one I'd put more trust in than yourself. I only doubt things are as desperate as you imagine. A great noise can be made by shallow waters. But if 'twill set your mind at ease I'll run you to Silvermines as soon as I've had another cup of tea."

"Oh, thanks, Chris," Kate sighed with relief. "And then you can talk to Bobby yourself. He'll listen to you. Just tell him if he wants to be back in the play next week he mustn't walk again till his ankle's better."

"Right," Chris smiled, "but there's no need

to be worrying your head over him. If his ankle's as bad as you say it is, he'll hardly be in the humour for walking."

* * *

If Chris could have seen Bobby at that moment, though, he might have changed his mind. Using the hurley to lever himself up and clinging with one arm to the wire netting surrounding the mine shaft, Bobby was sliding the lower half of his body through the hole that had been cut into it, while Mary, who had climbed through ahead of him, slowed his descent with a hand on either side of his waist. Thus helped, he was able to land gently on his good foot and pull the hurley through the hole after him.

"Be careful," Mary warned. "The sides of the shaft could easy cave in."

"Lie flat on your stomach," Bobby said, managing rather awkwardly to do so himself. "That way we can look down without having all our weight on the edge."

But even though they hung their heads right over the mine shaft, they found they could see very little. Bobby picked up a stone, held it out as far as he could reach and let go.

Almost at once, there was an echoing plop, like the sound of a stone dropped into a well.

"The water's deep," Bobby announced, "and it comes quite far up the shaft. I don't see how they could hide anything down there."

He lay still, looking down into the darkness of the shaft. He no longer believed there was anything to be found there, but he was trying to summon up the energy to lever himself upright again. He was tired and disheartened. Suddenly, a weak ray of sunlight struck the edge of the shaft before the clouds smothered it once more and, in that second, Bobby had a glimpse of something like a thin thread running down the side of the shaft. Reversing the hurley so it was now the right way round, he began to use it to fish around the side of the shaft where he thought the thread had been. At first he hooked only air. Then he felt a tug, as if he had a fish on the end of his strange rod. He gave a shout.

"What is it?" Mary asked.

"There's something hanging," he said, "but I can't pull it over. It just slips off the end of the hurley."

"Stay still," Mary said, clambering over him and around the top of the shaft to the far side. A gorse bush hung out over the shaft and

Mary cautiously pushed the branches aside. Just below it a pit prop projected a little way out from the side of the shaft and around it was tied the end of a length of fine chain.

"I see it!" she shouted in excitement, bending over to pull on the chain.

"Take care!" Bobby warned, but he was too late. The soil around the top of the shaft crumbled away and Mary, with a scream of terror, fell forward.

*   *   *

"There it is," Kate said, pointing to the Casey's house, and Chris pulled the van to a stop outside the door.

They both jumped out and Kate knocked on the door. When there was no reply, she lifted the latch, just as Mrs Casey appeared in the small hallway.

"Where's Bobby?" Kate cried, without even returning Mrs Casey's greeting or introducing Chris, for the house seemed ominously silent.

"I don't know and that's the truth," Mrs Casey said, "I went down to the shops for a few messages and when I got back he was gone and Mary with him. Left the baby on his own, too, though he was sleeping like an angel and she knew I'd not be long. Still, 'tis not like Mary."

"He's gone back up to the mine!" Kate cried. "I know he has. Oh, hurry, Chris, hurry!"

"Hang on a minute, Bugsy," Chris said, but Kate was already gone, running in the direction of the church.

There was a car parked in the church square and just as Kate drew level with it she heard the sound of an approaching engine. Glancing over her shoulder, she saw Mr Mulcahy's pick-up truck turning towards her from the corner of the Dolla road. Instinctively she ducked, to put the parked car between her and the truck. As it came towards the church, she moved around the front of the bonnet so that she was crouched to the left of it while the pick-up truck passed by on its right. As it did so, for one sickening moment she saw again a face she had seen only once before, but would never forget: the face of a man with a black moustache and a smile like a snarl, the man who had looked at his watch while their car skidded off the road and up onto the ditch.

The truck swung around the church and off to the right towards Mr Mulcahy's house. Kate started to run in the direction of the flooded mine, but she was scarcely clear of the church when she saw the truck had not stopped at the house. It was climbing the turn onto the track leading to the mine buildings. Then she heard a scream. It was a scream of utter terror and it came from beyond the pick-up truck, somewhere above and beyond the mine buildings. Kate swerved to her right. She was heading away from the flooded mine now, towards the truck. She was running towards the man whose face had haunted her dreams, but the thought only made her run faster. There was somebody up there who might be Bobby and that somebody might be in terrible danger.

* * *

Mary clung in terror to the projecting pit prop, her body suspended in space above the flooded mineshaft. The chain she had been clutching when she fell tore at her hands and she knew she would not be able to keep her grip on the wooden prop for long, even if the end did not break with the strain.

"Hang on. I'm coming!" Bobby shouted frantically, as he crawled around the top of the shaft, dragging the hurley with him. He knew he must keep back from the edge or the two of them would drop like the stone he had thrown in earlier. When he was directly above the pit prop, he stretched out flat so that his weight would not cause the top of the shaft to cave in further. Then he leaned over and gripped Mary's wrists with both hands.

"Don't let go of the prop," he called urgently, for he knew if the full weight of her body was suddenly released he might not have the strength to hold her.

"Can you hang on a few seconds more," he asked, "while I let go with one hand?"

Mary's white face looked up at him for a moment and he hoped the jerk of her head was a nod. With his free hand, he quickly laid the hurley across the shaft just above the prop, with both its ends resting on the ground. Then he seized her other wrist once more.

"Now," he said, trying to sound as calm as the PT instructor at school. "Hang on for one last second and listen to me. I'm going to try to pull you up, but you're going to have to help me all you can. You can try taking the strain with your feet on the side of the shaft. Don't scrabble at it. Try to sort of walk up it with your feet flat against it. Or maybe you can cross your ankles over the chain as if it were a rope, though it'll hurt. But try to help me raise

you until you can get a knee on to the hurley.
Only don't let go with both hands at once. Try
this hand first," and he squeezed the wrist
nearest to him. "Are you ready?"

Again the head jerked and his insides
seemed to jerk too.

"Then, let go!"

He felt the sudden strain as her body swung
round to face the wall of the shaft. Then the
pull eased slightly as she got some sort of
purchase with her feet. He braced his own,
ignoring the twinge in his bad ankle.

"Now," he said, praying he could manage the
extra weight, "let go with the other hand!"

He felt as if his arms would be torn from
their sockets as Mary struggled to raise
herself and, even as he strained every muscle
to lift her, he could feel the upper part of his
body being dragged further and further over
the edge. Then Mary's white face appeared
over the top of the shaft and, with a final
violent struggle, she fell forward half on top of
him, the hurley falling away behind her.
There was a splash as it hit the surface of the
water and then silence.

Numb with pain and relief, he lay
exhausted, his eyes closed, only dimly aware
of the sound of a car engine coming closer.

Then he heard shouts. With a tremendous effort he raised his head and opened his eyes. Through the netting, as if in a nightmare, he saw the flushed face and white hair of Mr Mulcahy and, beside him, a man with a black moustache whose eyes glittered with cold fury.

Bobby knew escape was impossible. He had lost his crutch and anyway they were trapped: trapped inside the circle of netting like animals in a cage.

* * *

Kate ran up the hillside until her breath clawed at her throat like an angry cat. Half way up, she suddenly saw a pair of horns rise up over a bush, followed by a black, whiskered face, but she never paused. She had more to fear now than goats.

She ran until she was above the mine buildings and, turning her back on them, ran on, guided by the distant sounds of the labouring truck engine, slamming truck doors, angry shouts and cries. Just as she knew she could run no further, the track began to fall away between high banks and she half-stumbled, half-fell down the hill, unable to pull up until she was brought to a stop by the side of the truck, parked across the junction at the bottom of the slope. She leaned against it for a second, gasping for breath, until she heard a voice from just beyond the bushes.

"I warned you yesterday," the voice said, and she recognised the deep, resonant voice of Mr Mulcahy. "I warned you to stay away from here — that it was dangerous. But you had to meddle with things that didn't concern you!"

Then she heard Bobby's voice, though at first she hardly recognised it, because it sounded strangely high and squeaky.

"If you harm us you'll be sorry," he said. "The Caseys know where we are!"

"Do they indeed," began Mr Mulcahy, but another voice, which filled Kate with terror, cut him short.

"We're only wasting time," it said. "I'm going in there to finish them off."

Kate heard the menacing sound of heavy boots and sprang forward, though she had no idea what she was going to do. Then she heard Bobby's voice again, in a last desperate attempt at bluff.

"The guards will be here any minute!" he cried. "My sister went to ring them ages ago."

Then, to her surprise, Kate heard her own voice shouting, loudly and clearly, as if she were not in the least out of breath: "This way, Sergeant! It's just the other side of those bushes!"

At the same moment, she heard the sound of a car racing up the top quarry road. Then something sprang from the bushes ahead of her and crashed into her, sending her sprawling.

9
You'll Never Miss the Water
Till the Well has Run Dry

hen Kate came to, she was lying on the couch in the Casey's kitchen. Her head hurt and for a moment she could not think where she was or how she got there. Then she remembered what had happened.

"Bobby!" she cried, and tried to struggle to her feet.

"Looking for me?" asked a familiar voice, and she saw Bobby, sitting in an easy chair with one leg resting on a stool. Mary was there too, shaking a rattle at the baby, who was gurgling delightedly in his pram.

Mrs Casey turned from the cooker at the sound of her voice.

"Stay quiet, child," she said. "The doctor says you're to rest yourself a while."

"I don't understand," Kate said. "What happened?"

"You had a fall and hit your head," Mrs Casey began, but Kate cut in.

"I didn't fall. I remember now. Someone pushed me. What happened to those men?"

"They ran away," Mary told her. "They thought it was the guards."

"You were brill!" Bobby chimed in excitedly. "When I saw Moustache starting to get through the hole in the netting I thought we were goners. He'd have made it look like we fell in, the way they did with that other boy."

"We nearly did!" Mary pointed out. "Me anyway!"

"If your father ever catches you next or near them mineshafts again he'll have your sacred life," her mother scolded.

"He will anyway," Mary said. "I took his hurley and it fell down the mineshaft."

Mrs Casey's mouth opened wide but before she could say anything Chris came in from outside.

"The guards are going up to examine the mineshaft now," he announced. "Anyone want to come?"

Everyone shouted "Me! Me!" and Chris grinned.

"I don't know about Bugsy Two," he said, going over to Kate. "You've a show to do tonight, remember. How d'you feel?"

"My head aches a bit," Kate admitted, "but I still don't know what happened."

"Bobby and Mary think they may have found the stolen picture in the shaft," Chris said. "But they nearly drowned themselves trying to get it so I said they must leave it to the guards."

"Did they get those men?" Mrs Casey asked anxiously. "I don't like the thoughts of them roaming the neighbourhood."

"They were seen running into Knockanroe Woods," Chris said, "but the guards have the mountain surrounded. The Sergeant says unless they had another car waiting on the Lackabrack Road they'd be sure to get them."

"But how did the guards know they were here?" asked Kate. "I only let on to have called them."

"Smartest thing you ever did," Chris said. "When they heard my van they must have thought it was the squad car and took to the hills. It was a while later the guards arrived, after Mrs Casey rang the station at Dolla."

"Let's go!" Bobby cried impatiently, hopping about on one foot. "We're missing everything!"

"Right so," Chris said, turning to follow.

"Please !" Kate begged. "Take me too!"

"I suppose since you're the heroine of the

hour we can't very well leave you," Chris said, "but you've got to take it easy. The doc said you might have dizzy spells. Here!" and he picked her up as if she were a bit of scenery and set her down gently in the van.

"But how did Mrs Casey know to ring the guards?" Kate persisted, as the van headed back up the road past the Mulcahy house. Whether it was due to the fall she did not know, but nothing seemed to be making sense.

"When you shot off that time, I started out after you," Chris explained, "but I was nearly flattened under a pick-up truck. It seemed to come out of nowhere and it was going like the clappers. Well, when I saw the guy in it was the same lad who did his best to make mincemeat out of us all on Sunday I lost my rag. Mrs Casey said that road behind the church was a cul-de-sac, so I took off after him in the van, while she rang the guards. I thought I'd see you on the way up, but you'd vanished."

"I took the short cut through the old mine workings," Kate explained. "It's quicker than the road. That's why I was there before you."

Chris pulled up beside the squad car that was parked on the dirt road leading up to the quarry. Mary tried to open the van door and winced.

"My arm still aches," she said.

"I'm not surprised," Chris remarked, getting out and opening the door for her. "From all I hear you gave a fair impersonation of a trapeze artist just now. I've three right crocks with me, so you're all to take it dead easy, d'you hear? Any risk-taking and back you go!"

The three crocks, having promised to do nothing foolish, helped each other down the steep track to where two uniformed men stood beside the second mineshaft. They had wound back the netting on one side and the younger of the two was using a boat hook to haul on the chain running down from the pit prop. As he walked backwards from the shaft, the loop of chain that lay on the ground grew bigger and bigger.

"There she blows!" cried the older man and Chris instinctively put a warning hand on Bobby's shoulder for fear he would forget his promise in the excitement, but Mary needed no holding back. One slip at the edge of the shaft had been enough.

As the end of the chain with its load was dragged clear of the shaft they all groaned with disappointment. The catch on the end of the line was only a wet and muddy fertiliser bag. Bobby and Kate had often seen them near Aunt

Delia's for, once their contents had been spread over the fields, they were used for bagging turf and the bags often sat for days or weeks in little clumps on the bog, awaiting collection by cart or lorry.

Sometimes at home they would use the bags as refuse sacks and they would sit along the Portobello Road awaiting the arrival of the bin men. Was it for a sackful of rubbish they had risked their lives?

The young garda looked doubtfully at the watching group and then at the Sergeant.

"I don't know should we open it and children present," he muttered. "It might contain the dismembered parts of a corpse maybe."

The Sergeant felt the bag and looked at the young garda as Kate's teacher looked at her when she was not paying attention in class.

"I never yet saw any part of a corpse that was rectangular and flat," he said scornfully. Then he took a clasp knife from his pocket and cut the sealed neck of the bag. From it, he pulled out a flat shape covered in bubblewrap.

"It *is* the picture!" Kate shouted. "It has to be!"

The Sergeant smiled. "Never count your chickens till they're hatched," he remarked dryly. While he cut the sticky tape holding the packaging in place and cautiously removed the wrapping, they all crowded around him.

It was a picture all right, though Kate could scarcely believe it was valuable. It was rather dark and gloomy, she thought, except for the central figure of a young woman. Dressed in poor, shabby clothes, she was seated on the ground, holding out an empty basket to a well-dressed man who seemed to have no interest in it, for he was already half-turned away, as if about to walk on. All around the woman, baskets were spread out on the ground. Some were large, some small; some were deep, some shallow; some had handles and some had none. Behind the woman, a man was riding by on horseback. He seemed to take no notice of an old woman nearby, whom Kate thought looked like a traveller. She had a small and grubby-looking child by the hand, and was clearly calling after the man on the horse. From her expression, Kate was sure that what she shouted was not a blessing but a curse.

The Sergeant nodded with satisfaction.

"The Basket Seller," he said. "There's small doubt of it!" And he tucked the bubblewrap around the picture again as tenderly as if he were wrapping a shawl around a baby.

"Is that it?" Kate asked him in surprise.

"I'd say 'tis," he replied, "but we'll know soon enough. Mr Flynn ought to be able to identify his own property. We'll see what he has to say about it. When we get back we'll want to have a few words with you young people about some of the things you've seen and heard since Sunday last. You'll be at the Casey's?"

"If you're not too long," Kate said.

"We have to be back in Limerick in good time for the show at the Belltable tonight," Chris explained. "We're in the cast."

"Are you now? Isn't it the great arts week we're having of it altogether, with paintings and actors thrown in?"

"And trapeze artists," Bobby chuckled.

The Sergeant looked puzzled.

"Don't mind him," Chris said. "He's a bit of a funny man."

"Right so." The Sergeant walked to the squad car, opened the boot and put the picture carefully into it. Then he turned to look back at the little group by the mineshaft. "We'll get you at the Casey's or the Belltable then," he called back by way of farewell.

"Or at Mrs Harris's Guesthouse on the Ennis Road," Chris called back, as the two men got into the squad car, turned it in the quarry and set off for Ballina.

"Is that really it?" Kate asked again. Somehow it seemed a tame ending to all their adventures.

"I don't know what you're complaining about," Bobby said. "You've got the show tonight."

"Which is why she must rest up now," Chris said firmly. "And if Bugsy the First thinks he's going to be back in the show by the time we open in Cork he shouldn't be prancing around on that ankle."

"I'm not putting my weight on it," Bobby insisted, hopping about on one foot to prove it, but Chris was not impressed.

"You're supposed to have it up on something," he said. "Come on, let's go!"

At that moment, they heard shouting in the woods higher up the mountain side and the sound of breaking branches.

"That must be the guards beating the woods for Moustache and Halo-head," Bobby said, turning to look up to the dark green of the plantation spruce beyond the straggle of ancient pine. Kate gave a little shiver.

"I hope they get them," she said.

Suddenly they heard the roar of an engine leaping into life close by. Chris spun round and started to run.

"Holy God!" he yelled. "The van!"

But even as he said it, the van swung in a crazy arc, its near wheels going up on the side of the ditch, and headed off down the dirt road.

"That way!" Kate shouted, and Chris swung right and plunged down the track running from the workings to the buildings and on to the village.

"If anything happens to that van Dad will go spare," Bobby said.

Blue uniformed men broke through the pine trees above them and started to lumber around the cut, heading for the church.

"I hope Chris doesn't catch up with them," Kate said, wishing for the second time she had kept her mouth shut.

"Don't worry, he won't!" Mary said. "They could be nearly half-ways to Dolla by now!"

A car horn blared below them and Mary, who had already reached the dirt road, let out a shriek of laughter. The others dragged themselves up the track to join her. From there they could see the road running down to the church and just above the church the van. It was stopped, with horn blaring, amidst a sea of struggling cattle.

"Batty Egan's bullocks!" Mary sobbed, helpless with laughter. "He must have been bringing them up to the top field."

The men in blue were converging on the car in an arc, with Chris out ahead. Then a squad car appeared on the road by the church.

"They had a road block on this side all the time," Kate cried.

"You bet!" Bobby agreed, "and now they've got them!"

But the bullocks, frantic at all the shouting and horn-blowing, were plunging about between and around the bonnets of both van and squad car, so the occupants of both were equally trapped. In the end it was the men on foot who reached the van first, having branched away from the track to drop down onto the empty road behind the van. At once Chris, whose milk collection lorries had often been stopped by cattle on the narrow roads of County Kerry, drove the frightened bullocks past the van till the gardai could wrench open the doors and overpower the fugitives.

Kate gave a long sigh of relief as she watched Mr Mulcahy and the man with the moustache being transferred to the squad car.

"That really is it now!" she said, satisfied.

But there was more. The Sergeant got back from Ballina with the news that the Flynns were delighted at the recovery of the painting.

Then the three of them told him everything that had happened, from the time the van had been driven off the road and up on the ditch. When Bobby came to the part about the car tracks running into the quarry, the Sergeant smiled.

"This young man has the makings of a detective," he said. "If he ever gets sick of the theatre, you never know but that there might be a career for him in the Garda Siochana."

So, when Chris and Kate had to leave for Limerick, Bobby had no complaints about being left behind once more.

"The Sergeant says they'll be pumping out the mine in the morning," he explained to them excitedly. "They've sent for the equipment and when it comes I'm going with them."

"Are you not even going to finish up the tour before starting on your new career?" Chris teased.

"Ah no, but I'm getting a lift up," Bobby replied importantly, "so I'll be there in case I can identify the car. I won't be walking at all, so it won't do my ankle a bit of harm. I'll be fit to play Cork, don't you worry!"

"I wasn't losing any sleep over it," Chris assured him.

And Kate lost no sleep either, even when the

Limerick Leader came out with a review of the play that had a flattering mention of her own performance. Of course, the name in the review was Bobby's, because that was what was printed in the programme, but Kate did not mind that. She knew that the critic had seen her and so did Pat.

And it was for Pat that the critic reserved his warmest praise, saying that the success of the whole play depended on his performance as the blind man. He wrote that Pat Masterson not only convinced him that he was blind, but that his other senses were heightened, so that he could sense a ghostly presence where others could not. That ought to put her father in good humour for at least a week, Kate thought.

Better still, after all his worrying, Chris too had a good notice, with the critic even saying that he was a young actor with a future. Kate felt sure her father would be in no hurry to replace him now.

She wondered if she should show the notice to Bobby, but he never asked about it, so she decided not to bother. All he could talk about, when the family arrived to collect him from the Casey's on Saturday, was the continuing drama at Silvermines. He had watched the level of water in the flooded mine falling, inch by inch, until the roof of the car broke the surface. And when the mechanical grab had finally lifted it clear of the water, he had been willing to swear that it was the self-same ice-blue Ford Sierra that had shot across in front of them on Sunday on the Limerick Road.

"More than likely," the Sergeant had agreed, after he had checked the engine number, "for it was stolen in Ballinasloe from outside a pub last Saturday night. The registration number's wrong, of course, but then it would be remarkable altogether if they hadn't the plate changed!"

While Bobby was telling the last of his adventures, Kate went to say goodbye to Mary. She could hardly believe that they had only known her for less than a week.

"Did your father eat you over the hurley?" Kate asked anxiously, for she knew what it was like to be in a father's bad books.

"He was mad at me at first," Mary said, "but he understood when I explained. And of course now I'll be able to get him another one!"

"That's great," said Kate, wondering what she meant.

Mary looked at her in surprise.

"Did Bobby not tell you?" she asked.

"Tell me what?"

"About the reward?"

Kate shook her head.

"The Sergeant says we're getting a reward from Mr Flynn for finding the picture."

"Wow!" said Kate. "I wonder what it will be."

"Money, the Sergeant said. We've to split it between the three of us. I asked him would my share be enough to get my Dad a new hurley and he said it would."

"It's not fair that you should have to pay for the hurley," Kate exclaimed. "I mean, it was for Bobby you took it. And it was Bobby and you found the picture, not me. I've had my reward, getting to play in Dad's company. Only for Bobby's ankle he mightn't have let me for yonks. And your Mum was real good to mind Bobby. I think you should have my share."

"Ah no," Mary said. "The Sergeant said there'd be plenty over after buying the hurley. He said there'd maybe even be enough for me to buy the dress I saw in the window of the boutique in Limerick the night we came to your show, *and* go shopping in Ellen Street Market for something as a present for Mum. But I'd love if you'd do something else for me, Kate."

"What?"

"Send me a postcard from Cork and the other places you go on the tour. So I know how the play's going and that. I mean, it's going to be a bit boring when you go."

"I will of course," Kate said. "Tell you what. Maybe in the Christmas holidays when the company's in Dublin your Mum and Dad would let you come and stay with us for a few days."

"Oh, that'd be great," Mary said.

"Come on, Kate!" Maggie called. "There's still a show to be played tonight, you know."

"I'll write," Kate promised, as she got into the back of the car beside Bobby.

"Wish me luck in Cork!" Bobby shouted to Mary and she shouted back: "Good Luck! Good Luck!" as the car made a U-turn in the main street and headed back towards the main Nenagh-Limerick Road.

"And this is where it all began," thought Kate, as for the last time they drove past the lay-by on the right and the steep hill running down to Cappadine on the left. "But I'm glad it did. Because only for that I'd never have met Mary or got to be Bugsy the Second, and it's still my part for tonight, anyway!"